"Actually, there's [illegible] ned I need to pass on."

"Yeah?" Bryce sat up.

"Before we visited that family, she gave me notice that there's more than one family around here with unmarried young ladies."

"Well, that's to be expected," Bryce said with a snort.

"I guess. I just never thought about it," Logan admitted. "Truth is, Hattie said they don't get a lot of visitors up this way."

"Coulda told you that by the almost-empty train." Bryce lay back down. "That's what makes it an adventure."

"Still, she was saying they don't meet new men very often, especially well-established bachelors."

"Stands to reason."

Logan could tell the exact moment Bryce got it, because he shot up like his pallet was covered in fire ants.

"You mean they'll be makin' eyes at *us*?" Alarm and disbelief painted Bryce's question.

"Yep." Logan made use of Bryce's favorite answer.

"Did Hattie tell us what to do about it?" Bryce did his best to pace around the loft, without much luck.

"Just watch what we say so we don't put any ideas into their heads."

"Sounds to me like they had ideas before we even got here!" Bryce walked into the bench, banging his shin and sloshing water onto the floor. He sank back down onto his pallet and used one of the hand towels to mop up the spill.

"Take it easy. Hattie just thought we deserved advance notice. Don't spend time alone with any of 'em, is all." Logan blew out the lantern and pulled up the covers.

Bryce groaned. "Sounds to me like this is gonna be more of an adventure than we reckoned."

"I'll watch your back," Logan bargained. "You watch mine."

KELLY EILEEN HAKE has loved reading her whole life, and as she grew older, she learned to express her beliefs through the written word. Currently, she is a senior in college working toward her BA in English. She intends to earn her Single Subject Credential so she can share her love of words with high school students! She likes to cook, take walks, go to college group activities at her church, and play with her two dogs, Skylar and Tuxedo.

Books by Kelly Eileen Hake

HEARTSONG PRESENTS
HP640—Taking a Chance

Chance Adventure

Kelly Eileen Hake

Heartsong Presents

To my mother, who has supported me through every word I've written since I learned the alphabet and encouraged me to pursue a career in writing. Without her guidance, patience, wisdom, and passed-on love of literature, this book wouldn't exist. Thank you, Mommy. I love you.

The herbs mentioned in this book were carefully researched and authentic to the era. Some have since been found to be questionable or even dangerous. In no way do I advocate the use of any herb, medication, or curative without checking first with your medical doctor.

A note from the Author:
I love to hear from my readers! You may correspond with me by writing:

Kelly Eileen Hake
Author Relations
PO Box 719
Uhrichsville, OH 44683

ISBN 1-59789-005-7

CHANCE ADVENTURE

Our mission is to publish and distribute inspirational products offering exceptional value and biblical encouragement to the masses.

All scripture quotations are taken from the King James Version of the Bible.

PRINTED IN THE U.S.A.

one

Logan Chance rubbed his sore legs and groaned before pulling off his boots. Hard days in the saddle had never fazed him before his older brothers all suddenly decided to make him an uncle. Not four years ago, the six Chance men had had their hands full with just Polly and Ginny Mae—or so they'd thought. Now, thanks to Miriam, Alisa, and Delilah, they sported no fewer than nine little bundles of joy. It would be ten any day now—not counting the McPhersons' growing brood, which ended up on Chance Ranch more often than not. Seventeen children, and each one demanding a "horsie" ride from Uncle Logan as soon as they could talk.

No wonder Logan was restless—he didn't even have a wife, and he was already tied down! He rubbed his neck as the door opened and Bryce came in, bringing with him a gust of rain-soaked wind and muddy boots smelling of the stables. They were the last two bastions of bachelorhood, he and Bryce. If they didn't watch out, they'd be trapped just like their other four brothers. With all the womenfolk around, you never knew what new female would pop up with a smile on her face and a bare ring finger. After all, that's just what had happened to Gideon, Titus, Paul, and even surly old Daniel.

Not that he didn't love each and every fuzzy head and gummy smile, but Logan ached for some excitement before he gave in to the inevitable. After all, his brothers had waited until they were years older than he was now, and all of those years had been spent in a man's world of riding, ranching, hunting, and building. Logan just wanted some of the same, but there was no way he'd find it at Chance Ranch. It was 1874, and the world was growing so fast there was no end to the adventures out there.

"What's got you lookin' so serious?" Bryce's voice interrupted Logan's thoughts.

"Awww. . .nothin'." It was one thing to think about his dissatisfaction but entirely another to give voice to it.

Bryce pinned him with a level stare. "When're you goin' to admit that it's getting to you?"

"What do you mean?"

"You're chomping at the bit here, so why don't you go and do something about it?"

Logan shook his head in disbelief. Bryce, so often oblivious and awkward socially, still surprised him with his uncanny ability to see straight into his head. "Like what?"

"I don't know, but it seems to me that if you don't set out soon, you never will. You'll be needed for the calving season, but the end of spring would be a good time to go stretch your legs and satisfy your curiosity."

Logan mulled that over for a minute. "And what about the Chance vote?" If the others didn't want him to go, the situation could get ugly.

"Seems to me this isn't a voting issue. You may be the youngest, Logan, but you're not a boy any longer. Men make their own decisions, and since this one won't hurt the ranch, everyone will respect that." Bryce spoke with an authority Logan was unaccustomed to hearing from him.

"You think it'll be that easy, huh?" He flopped down onto his unmade bunk and shoved his boots underneath.

"Nothing worthwhile ever came easy, Logan. If I were you, I'd start praying."

❧

"Get up."

Logan awoke with a start when a wadded-up sock hit him smack-dab on the nose. Giving a huge yawn, he lobbed it back at his brother, who caught it easily and stuck it on his foot.

"What? Breakfast bell hasn't even rung yet." He pulled up his blankets farther around his neck and scowled at Bryce.

"I know." Bryce looked annoyingly alert already. "Unless you dreamed up a plan last night while you were sleeping, you've got to nail down some particulars before breakfast."

Logan scratched the stubble on his chin. "What for? I haven't even made up my mind to go yet. No rush."

Bryce snorted. "You've got to tell everyone as soon as you can, get them used to the idea. Best try it in the morning when Gideon, Daniel, and Titus are a little groggy."

Seeing the logic in Bryce's advice, Logan sat up and started running through options. "Where should I say I'm goin'?"

"San Francisco? Big growing city like that'll give you plenty of opportunities."

"Nah." Bryce obviously wasn't thinking big enough. "I don't want to be a city slicker—what's the fun in that? Besides, it's too close to really count as an adventure."

"So you want someplace that's not too civilized and not too close?" Bryce summarized.

"Yep."

"Any other requirements?"

"I should know something about the place before going in."

"That's a mighty tall order, but I think I know just the place." Bryce looked mighty pleased with himself, but he didn't say another word.

"Well?" Logan prodded.

"Sounds to me like you're going to Salt Lick Holler." With that, Bryce walked out the door, leaving Logan to scramble into his clothes and tromp after him to the breakfast table.

As the women looked after the children and the men started making plans for the day's labor, Logan tried to recall all he knew of Salt Lick Holler.

The MacPherson brothers, known more commonly as Obie, Hezzy, and Mike, owned a spread neighboring Chance Ranch but hailed from Hawk's Fall. When they tried en masse to court Delilah—long before she wed Paul—she cleverly encouraged them to write back home for brides. They couldn't think of any girls from Hawk's Fall, but Mike remembered girls from the neighboring Salt Lick Holler. So Lovejoy had hauled Eunice, Lois, and her sister, Tempy, from Salt Lick to Reliable to wed them off. Somehow she wound up filling the hole in Daniel's heart.

They were all upstanding people with an easy freedom Logan envied. They'd settled well here but kept ties back to the holler—Lovejoy, in particular, wrote to their healer. It was far enough away to be a journey, foreign enough to be an exploration, but vouchsafed so the Chance clan wouldn't protest. Salt Lick Holler was perfect.

❧

Salt Lick Holler was far from perfect, but it was home, and Hattie Thales loved it. She took a deep breath of crisp mountain air tinged with the scent of freshly fallen rain. Spring had come again, bringing along with it the promise of new life.

Spring meant she'd be needing to shore up her stock of medicines. She'd have use for black haw bark, motherwort, cramp bark, and fennel seed before long. Hattie didn't know what meant more work for her—the babes born after a cold winter, or the scrapes and sprains collected by men and young'uns jumping around like crickets to be outside again. Come to think of it, she'd best keep an eye out for any golden seal, heal-all, and larkspur.

Widow Hendrick had taught her all the yarbs and medicines she knew, so Hattie would be ready. Her favorite part of healing was walking through the lush country in search of yarbs, roots, and berries to put in bags, vials, teas, and poultices for later use. This winter she'd even received lessons in reading and writing, which she'd taken to like a duck to water. She'd come far in the past two years.

Who would have figured Hattie Thales would ever be so book-learned? Not her pa, who'd wed her off to Horace Thales as soon as she'd become a woman. Horace had been a good man, but he'd boasted more than twice her years and less than half her joy in life. For six years she'd fetched, cooked, mended, cleaned, and carried for him with nary a word of thanks for any of her trouble. Then a widow-maker deadwood branch had fallen on her husband and crushed the life from them both.

He hung on nigh a year, and she nursed his body but couldn't touch his bitter heart. As his health declined, so did the life Hattie had built for herself. She carried out all her household duties, stayed faithful to Horace, and tried to make him comfortable, but nothing she did could make up for the way she'd failed him. He knew he was fixing to leave this world, but he had no one to pass his name to before he died. Horace never said a word, but that bitter knowledge tainted the very air around them.

It had been over a year since he'd passed on, and Hattie could have married again—but no decent man would have her. She didn't hold it against them. Who could blame them for wanting sons? A body couldn't deny nature's way: The woman brought forth children, and the man provided for them all. Once a woman lost a babe the way Hattie had, she'd never be able to carry another. Her miscarriages didn't only mean she'd failed as a woman; they meant that any husband of hers wouldn't have the chance to be a man in the eyes of his kith and kin.

So she'd left her home to a new couple just starting out with every hope in the world and moved in with Widow Hendrick. Miz Willow, as Hattie had come to call the elderly healer, had outlived everyone she'd known so far and was glad for the company. Besides, since Lovejoy Linden had fetched her sister and the Trevor gals out to Reliable and landed herself a Chance husband, somebody needed to tend to the health of the holler. If Miz Willow had her way, she'd be around forever and a day, but the older woman needed more help as her capable hands grew stiff from rheumatism and her back twisted with age.

Hattie spotted some burdock and stooped to dig up some of the root. It helped with joint pain, and she'd used up most of her supply this winter. The cold always brought aches to the older folks. She'd need some devil's claw root for Miz Willow's rheumatism, too.

The sun hid behind a heavy cloud, casting the meadow into shadow. It seemed as though they were in for another shower. Hattie hurried to gather as much of the precious root as she could without killing the plant. She tucked it into her gathering bag and turned back toward home.

As she made it to the door, the heavens opened. She stomped her feet on the threshold to loosen the mud, then stepped inside and shut the door before taking off the worn boots. She hung up her cape and carried her gathering pouch over to where Miz Willow sat in her old rocker.

"I was askeered you wasn't gonna make it in time," she chided. "M' bones say it'll be a gully warsher for shore."

"And I know those bones o' yourn never tell tales." Hattie bent down and gave the old woman a kiss on her leathery cheek. "I'll fix you some devil's claw tea to ease the ache." She busied herself with the old kettle and added more wood to the fire.

"Thankee, child." Only Miz Willow could call a twenty-one-year-old widow-come-healer a child and give no offense. "I'm a-fixin' to write a letter for Lovejoy. Roads oughta be openin' agin soon. Anythin' we'll be a-needin' from them parts?"

Hattie thought for a moment, picturing the jars and vials of the storeroom in her mind's eye. "Not much. I harvested devil's claw and burdock today and have my eye on a patch of motherwort and some fennel. Could use more of the mule's ear root for Otis's rheumatiz. Wouldn't turn down some witch hazel, iff'n she cain spare it. I have plenty of rusty rye to trade."

She waited while the widow painstakingly scrawled out the list, pen clasped tightly between her pale fingers. There was a time when Hattie would have envied Lovejoy her good fortune in finding a husband despite her barren womb, but Lovejoy's marriage had given Hattie a place and purpose back in the holler. Hattie could only thank the good Lord for the gifts He'd seen fit to give her. She had a home and a respectable living. She'd never want for food or warmth, and she'd touch the life of every child in the holler even though she'd never have one of her own. What more could a body want?

two

Adventure. It loomed on the horizon, as glowing and enticing as the setting sun. It beckoned to him, and Logan nudged Britches to trot so he could present his plan to the family.

The gelding had earned his name by being pure white up to his rump and hindquarters, where the white gave way to a rich chestnut brown. Logan's father had given Bryce the runt to nurse back to health if he could. Bryce's calm voice and gentle care had seen the pony through, though he would never be a large horse. Since Logan was the youngest brother and had the shortest legs, it made sense for him to ride Britches at the time. Now, years later, it was an undeniable fact that Logan had gotten too big for his Britches.

But the horse was loyal and shared his rider's love of open spaces, cool streams, and fast runs. Logan could have his pick of any horse on the ranch, but he couldn't bring himself to leave behind a companion that had served him so well—same as he'd stayed on the ranch for the past two years even though it had become increasingly obvious he was a round peg surrounded by square holes.

At least he wouldn't have to worry that Britches would be put out to pasture when he left. Mike MacPherson, the smallest of the MacPherson brothers, had an affinity for the horse and had been dropping hints lately. They'd be a good fit together. It never hurt to keep one's relatives happy, and Mike was his brother's wife's sister's husband, after all.

Yep. Logan's family tree had grown as tangled as Polly's

hair when he'd tried to braid it yesterday. It had taken Delilah and Lovejoy the better part of the afternoon to straighten out that mess. The fact that he'd been reduced to messing with a little girl's hair proved he needed a change of pace.

He hadn't brought up the issue at breakfast—he'd needed some time in the saddle to think it over. He was already known as the loose cannon in the family, so he had to be as logical and serious as possible when he brought up the plan. If it sounded like he was just going off half-cocked, the family would veto his plan. After all, he was the youngest brother, and they might not take to his suggesting he leave them in California to travel across the country.

Now he knew how he'd broach the subject.

Logan slid out of the saddle and led Britches into the barn. As he removed the horse's tack, rubbed him down, brushed him, and gave him water and hay, Logan reviewed his plan of attack once more. It was crucial to wait until everyone had eaten their fill. Knowing everyone would feel warm and full after a long day's work, he figured the end of supper would be the best time to bring it up.

First, he had to wait until an opportunity presented itself. It might take a couple of days, but this was important enough for him to be patient. He'd ease into it on the sly by asking Lovejoy how things were back at the holler and what it was like this time of year. She was bound to talk about how beautiful it was and say something about one of the folks back there to make them all laugh. With everyone smiling and off guard, he'd casually mention how he'd like to see it for himself. Bryce would back him up. Then everyone would realize he meant it. The whole thing should go off without a hitch.

Hattie woke up early in the morning to the *pitter-pat-plink* of rain striking the wood and tin roof. She stretched carefully so as not to wake Miz Willow asleep in the bed beside her, then snuggled deeper beneath the warm covers.

Once more she reveled in the way their home boasted no leaks. Growing up, she'd helped Mama put pots and jars beneath the tiny streams of water pouring in from the roof. She remembered wondering if they'd reach far enough to find one another and become one long fall of water. When she'd wed Horace, she'd slept in a true, above-the-ground bed for the very first time. The Thales's cabin was a far cry from Papa's shack, but tiny drips still found their way through the walls and under the door, muddying the floor.

But the healers' hut was something else altogether. Vern Spencer had been a prideful man. A woodsmith by trade, he determined to have the best home in the whole holler. To that end, the place even had the luxury of two rooms. The offshoot served as the healers' storeroom now, and the other held the fireplace, table, and bed for everyday living. It was one of the soundest buildings standing in the holler. The only thing that weathered the storms of life any better was old Miz Willow herself.

The rain petered out, and Hattie eased out of the bed. She pulled on her overdress and stockings before stoking the fire and putting on a kettle for morning tea. She was just starting to fry the eggs when a knock sounded at the door.

"Mornin', Nessie," Hattie said, ushering the visitor inside. "What cain I do for you?"

"Pa's feelin' poorly agin' and sint me ta fetch some a yore medicine." Nessie kept her head down, refusing to look Hattie in the eye.

Rooster was feeling the effects of his brew again. Drink held that man in its grip tight as could be. Peddlin' moonshine to other fools was only the beginning of the things for which he'd have to answer to the good Lord on

Judgment Day. The way she'd dealt with her father made Lovejoy Linden—now Lovejoy Chance—an even more amazing woman.

"Nessie, look at me."

The girl barely peeked up before returning her gaze to the floorboards, but it was enough to prove Hattie's fears.

"He was samplin' his own wares again, was he?" Hattie knelt down and pushed Nessie's hood back off her face to get a better look at the purple bruise coloring the girl's left cheek.

Nessie nodded wordlessly. Rooster Linden had gotten worse in the past year, but it seemed there wasn't a thing anybody could do about it. He'd always been unpredictable after drink, but lately he'd tended more to angry and violent. Hattie got up and went to the storeroom and came back with a poultice of marshmallow and burdock root.

"This should holp with the swellin' and soothe the skin a bit." Hattie paused but had to ask. "Did he hit you anywhere else?" At the shake of Nessie's head, she said, "I'm powerful sorry he took out his wrath on you. You ken 'tisn't yore fault?"

"Yes, thankee." Nessie cleared her throat. "Cain I have Pa's medicine now?"

Hattie rocked back on her heels and prayed. *Lord, I want to do Yore will, but I don't know what that is. Mr. Linden's hurtin' himself and others. As a healer, I'm s'posed to holp wherever I cain—but iff'n I make it so his drinkin's easier, who does that really holp? Not Nessie or even Rooster. But iff'n I don't, he'll be riled as a bear and drink more. Then Nessie'll suffer his anger agin. How do I protect her?*

"Here you go, Nessie." Miz Willow took the decision from Hattie's hands by handing a packet to Nessie. "That'll clean him out right quick, though he won't thank me for it 'til after."

"Thankee, Widow Hendrick." Nessie shrugged her hood back on.

"Wait a minute. Have some of this." The older woman passed the girl a mug of tea. "It'll keep yore bones warm on the walk back. And when yore pa feels better, you make shore you ask him to come down and visit with Widow Hendrick." A steely glint lit her usually twinkling eyes. "We have sommat to discuss, him and me."

❧

Logan breathed deeply as he stepped into the main cabin. *Smells like pot roast, mashed potatoes, and could that possibly be...*

"Muck!" Alisa's voice interrupted his thoughts. He was surprised to see her tapping her tiny foot and glaring up at him. "Go wipe off your boots, Logan. I just cleaned the floor!"

He obligingly loped back out the door, stomped his feet, and came back in. Little things like that didn't seem like much, but he heard those kinds of remarks every day. "Wipe your feet." "Don't put your boots on the chair." "Hold the baby for a minute." "Not like that!" "Why aren't you washed up yet?" "How'd you get these so dirty?" "Where'd you put the. . .oh, never mind." "*Another* hole to mend?" The endless refrain was enough to set a man's teeth permanently on edge.

He spotted the apple pies he'd been smelling earlier and reconsidered. Having women around wasn't all bad. It definitely had its compensations! His mouth watering, Logan filched a biscuit from one of the baskets, only to have his knuckles rapped with a wooden spoon.

"Ow!" He dropped it like a red-hot poker.

"You know better than that, Logan Chance." Miriam shook the wooden spoon at him.

There was a time when he would've flashed her a smile, waited until she turned around, then crammed it into his mouth while she wasn't looking. Now it wasn't worth it. The mischief had been all but scrubbed and chided out of him. Things had come to a sorry state indeed.

He took a seat and bowed his head for the prayer, then shoveled forkfuls of meat and potatoes into his mouth while everybody chattered away. Chomping on a buttery biscuit so light it could've flown, Logan promised himself he'd ignore the domesticity of it all and enjoy his family before he set out. When plates of apple pie came around, Logan judged the time was right.

"So have you had any letters from Widow Hendrick lately?" He addressed the question to Lovejoy before trying the pie. The taste of cinnamon and apples lingered as sweet as victory while Lovejoy started speaking about the holler.

"As a matter of fact, had one jist this week. Seems the spell of whooping cough is over—they lost two young'uns and one older fella." She shook her head sadly.

This wasn't going the way he'd hoped. He tried to steer the conversation into more pleasant territory. "Could've been much worse. How's everybody else doin'?" He held his breath until she smiled.

"Well, there're at least three babes on the way for this spring, so Hattie's busy harvesting and offered to send me some rusty rye." She paused for a moment before continuing. "Isn't it just like the good Lord to send three new lives after taking the same number? Keeps it all in balance."

"Balance?" Logan jumped on his opportunity. "Seems to me they're a bit short over there since Reliable snatched Obie, Hezzie, Mike, Eunice, Lois, Tempy, and yourself."

"Now if that doesn't just prove it, I don't know what will, Logan. See, God sent out three men, but the loss of eligible bachelors would've been hard to bear, so He paved the way for their brides, too." She beamed across the table as all the women nodded in agreement, Paul nudging Delilah with his elbow.

"I just meant that Salt Lick Holler's sent a bunch of wonderful people out to Reliable"—Logan leaned back to appear nonchalant—"but Reliable hasn't returned the favor."

"There's some truth to that." Daniel put an arm around his wife's shoulders. "We're keeping 'em, too."

Murmurs of agreement sounded around the table, punctuated by one of the babies banging a spoon against the table. If Logan didn't do something immediately, the conversation would be over and he'd 've lost his chance.

"I bet it's nice this time of year." He shrugged and gobbled the last bite of his pie.

"Shore is." Lovejoy's eyes went a little dreamy. "You cain smell things a-growin' from the earth in spring. It's fresh and green. Birds sang at ya; butterflies flit around through the air. The sun's so bright, you walk under the trees to keep cool until a breeze picks up. Baby critters pop their tiny heads up around every corner, and the sounds of life rustle alongside the ring of wood bein' chopped." She gave a wistful sigh. "At night the stars glow like it's their last time, and glowworms dart 'round the trees an' ruffle yore hair iff'n ya git too close. It'll be that way 'til the middle of summer."

"Oh, Lovejoy, that sounds beautiful." Alisa reached over to pat her on the arm.

"I'd like to see all that," Logan burst in before Lovejoy could start assuring them all how wonderful Chance Ranch was and how she'd rather be here anyway.

"Everybody should." Lovejoy smiled at him. "But it's a better place ta visit than ta call home."

"I've already got a home. Seems like I'm missing a place to visit." Logan sent up a little prayer. "Would that be possible?"

"You mean it, don't you?" Delilah looked at him in surprise.

" 'Course he doesn't. He's got everything he could want right here." Gideon brushed the idea away like a pesky gnat, and Logan felt his freedom slipping away.

three

"I don't know about that." Every head turned toward Bryce.

"What are you talking 'bout, Bryce?" Daniel drew Lovejoy closer.

"I'm just saying we all remember moving out here to start Chance Ranch, making a home and a place for ourselves with Ma. Logan was barely eight, though. It makes sense he'd like to stretch his legs and take in a few sights before he settles down." Bryce cast a meaningful look around the table at all the children.

"There is something about being in a new place that makes a person learn to follow God's will and grow into oneself." Delilah spoke thoughtfully, obviously thinking of the time she'd spent in San Francisco to sell her art. While away from Chance Ranch, she'd found God.

"You've got a point. Stickin' where things is familiar ain't always what's best." Lovejoy grinned at Daniel, who relaxed a bit.

"I don't see why it wouldn't be an option after calving," Titus offered.

"Me, neither," Paul agreed. "I think it might be a nice change of pace for everyone—we'll get to hear all about what you get into instead of having to witness it and pull you out of it!" Everyone laughed.

"I don't suppose you two could get into too much trouble," Daniel assented.

"Two?" Logan had missed something, he was sure.

"Yeah." Gideon jerked a thumb toward Bryce. "Like he

said, you guys have grown up here. You both need the experience of making your own way in the world for a while."

"Whoa. How'd I get dragged into this?" Bryce held out his hands, palms up, as though trying to shove away a skunk without getting sprayed.

"Oh, come on," Titus chortled. "You two are like Frick 'n' Frack. Always have bin."

Logan kept his trap shut and thought about it. Of all his brothers, Bryce understood him the best and bothered him the least. He'd be fairly quiet, and besides, he usually went along with whatever Logan decided anyway. Plus, it was a six-day trip, and he could use some company on the way. Sounded good to him.

"We'd feel more comfortable with two of you going," Alisa encouraged Bryce.

"I'll send off the letter tomorrow making arrangements," Lovejoy determined. "There's not a moment to lose!"

"Time for an official vote." Gideon called them to order. "All in favor of Bryce and Logan visiting Salt Lick Holler for the summer after the calving season, put up your hands."

Logan watched everyone vote for his adventure and gave Bryce an apologetic smile as he followed suit. It was settled. They'd both go.

❧

"Wait, Hattie!" Hattie turned to see Nate Rucker rushing up to her.

"Was thar sommat else I should know 'bout the babe, Mr. Rucker?" Hattie's smile fled. Abigail Rucker was due any week now, and Hattie had taken to checking up on the woman almost every day. She seemed fine when Hattie left her just moments ago.

"Nah. Abigail and I are beholden to you for yore care. Yore a fine healer." He put his hands on his knees to catch his breath. "It's jist that thar's a letter for you and Widow Hendrick. I plumb fergot about it on account of the babe."

He handed her a slightly smudged envelope. Hattie recognized the fancy paper and loopy print as being from Lovejoy.

"Thankee for yore quick memory, Mr. Rucker."

"Welcome. I've gotta go, but I'll be seein' ya afore long." He gave a jaunty wave and turned back, leaving Hattie to her thoughts.

It was Nate and his wife's first babe, scarcely a year into their marriage. They'd moved into Hattie's old home when she went to live with Miz Willow. Now the place would have the child she'd never been able to bear. It would be a real home. Such bittersweet thoughts, but at least she'd have a hand in bringing the babe into the world. That was something to make her give thanks.

"How's Abigail Rucker doin' this fine spring day?" Miz Willow asked as soon as Hattie stepped inside.

"Restless as a raccoon in a river, but farin' well." Hattie smiled and brought out the envelope. "I've got sommat for you!"

A grin broke across the widow's face, deepening the lines given to her by years of honest living and laughter. "How nice. How 'bout you read it to me. It'd be good practice."

Hattie slid a finger beneath the corner of the delicate paper and lifted open the glued flap of the envelope. She pulled out the sheet of paper, unfolded it, and carefully shaped the words with her mouth as she read it aloud:

Dear Miz Willomena and Hattie,

Praise be that th' whooping cough has ended. I keep you in my prayers ev'ry day. Thankee for the valerian root you sent. Little Polly says it holped with 'er head poundin's. Yore so good to us.

Night past, we was talkin' 'bout how much Salt Lick Holler has sent down to Reliable, and we come ta the truth that we ain't returned the favor. Important as it is to keep strong ties with yore kin, we wish to rectify our negligence. (Lookie thar—Delilah learned me that word. Means we ain't been watchin' out like we should.)

Hattie stumbled over the bigger words and sounded out the new one. "Well, live and learn. That thar's a fancy phrase."

The widow was obviously pleased with both her students—Lovejoy for making good use of her lessons, and Hattie for learning them.

"You want I should keep on?" Hattie wondered if Miz Willow would like to read the letter herself, seeing as how it was a real link between her and her friend. Letters were special, something to touch and still almost hear a voice, too.

"Please do."

Tempy an' Lois are expectin' again, so's none of us cain come down. 'Sides, we don't know what good could come a leavin' all the young'uns with Obie, Hezzie, and Mike. So's the best we cain send you is our love.

But Logan and Bryce Chance (Dan's least brothers) are fine young lads with God in thar hearts and adventure in thar eyes.

Hattie paused as she saw the next line, then kept on.

Iff'n yore agreeable, they'd like to visit come end of spring thru summer. Bryce charms anything with fur or feathers, and Logan does better with folks with two legs. I was thinkin' they could sleep in yore barn, and in return for their keep, they'd be happy to holp any way they could—huntin', fishin', buildin', choppin', an' such.

Pray on it. You both have to be fine with it. I know Hattie's still a bonnie young lassie, so's it may be awkwart ta have them around her. They're right respectful bucks, but none of ourn want to impose. All our love regardless of yore decision.

Forever yores,
Lovejoy Chance

"Well, I'll be." Miz Willow just rocked in her chair, looking thoughtful.

Hattie didn't venture much of an opinion but pointed out, "That's jist a few weeks from now, I'd imagine."

"True, true. We'd hafta git ready mighty quick." The widow caught her gaze. "Iff'n you say it's fine by you."

Rather than just agree as the widow obviously wanted, Hattie thought about it for a minute. She'd gone through so much change in the last two years and finally settled here. She had everything she could want and praised God for it. Did she really want two young men stepping into their lives and setting the whole holler aflutter?

It wasn't her first choice, but then again, it wasn't her decision. It was Miz Willow's. Besides, there was plenty to keep her busy and out of their way.

"No skin off my nose, Miz Willow. I cain think on a few gals who'd be mighty pleased to hear 'bout two new fellas comin' for a visit."

Widow Hendrick nodded. "And I know Silk Trevor will want ta know the type of folks who've taken her nieces into their family. Come to think on it, so do I." She rocked a bit more and reached for a pencil and paper. "So do I."

❧

The barbed wire bit through the tough leather the moment Logan looked away. He tugged the glove off with his teeth and sucked on his finger 'til the bleeding stopped, then kept right on mending the fence.

Served him right for daydreaming on the job. He'd been wondering what the mountains were like, whether the train would feel as quick as a fast gallop, if all the folks in Salt Lick Holler would sound like Lovejoy—gentle and kind of musical. What did the men do to pass the time? How did everyone make a living?

He'd know the answers soon enough, but for now he needed to keep his thoughts on the work at hand. Otherwise he'd end up like Paul—everyone knew back in his courting days that he'd fallen off his horse and broken his arm because he was busy thinking about Delilah. *Well, at least I'm not being distracted over a woman.*

He heard Bryce coming before he saw the horse and winced. They'd started in the middle, and both were supposed to reinforce two miles' worth of the safeguard. Logan blamed his slow pace on his oft-pricked fingers.

Bryce swung out of the saddle and came over to help him finish up. They worked side by side until the job was done. Not a word passed between them. After they finished, they sat and guzzled some lukewarm water from their canteens.

"How long you gonna be mad at me for something I had no control over?" Logan decided it was time to clear the air. Bryce had been even quieter than usual the past month—ever since the Chance clan had decided they'd both go to Salt Lick Holler if the Widow Hendrick and Hattie Thales let them.

Bryce blinked, then drew his bandanna across his forehead. "I'm not mad at you, Logan."

"Then why've you been so all-fired quiet lately?"

"I've never been much of a talker. You know that."

"But you always talked to me." Logan grumbled this, not

wanting to sound too whiny.

"What's done is done, little brother." Bryce slugged him on the shoulder. "It's not what either of us thought it'd be, but I won't be the hitch in your plans."

"Thanks." Logan's voice went gruff as he thought about how his brother was willing to take this trip for him, even though Bryce would always be happy to stay at home—well, in the barn, anyway. "I'm glad that's settled." He got up and dusted off his seat.

"Who says it's settled?" Bryce grinned as they went back for their horses. "Maybe they won't want us."

"Now why would you say something that crazy?" Logan grinned and waggled his eyebrows. "Who wouldn't want us?"

four

Dear Lovejoy and Chance Family,

Sorry bout my writin—I'm new at it but Miz Willow says I don't git nough times to practice, so here goes.

We're glad the valerian roots holped Miss Polly's head and have sent more along with some rusty rye. Already used some of this batch last year on one of Silk Trevor's daughters—Katherine. She's delivered of a healthy son an she says to make shore I tole you to tell Obadiah MacPherson she's named her chile after him. She says Hezzie and Mike 're next since she's done run outta names from her man's kin.

Everyone's all aflutter here bouts since we tole em how Logan and Bryce'll be comin. We figgur iff'n y'all write back rite quick we'll know they're comin bout a week afore they git here in the end of May. Sowry we cain't offer nuthin better'n a barn for 'em, but I'll clean out the loft and make it as nice as I cain. Miz Willow reckons a barn were good nuff for Jesus Hisself so it'll do jist fine.

We cain't hardly wait to meet you boys! Everyone's excited. The mensfolk plan on takin you hunting and the women want to have a doin's to celebrate yore arrival, but Widow Hendrick tole em they'd hafta wait til yore a bit more settled.

God be with you all.

Truly Yores,
Hattie Thales and Willomena Hendrick

Logan gave a whoop as Lovejoy finished reading the news, then reached for the letter. He reread it quickly and gave a silent prayer of thanksgiving.

Lord, it wasn't easy coming to this decision, much less convincing the others to support it. You've warned that the road we are to follow is narrow and hard, not simple. But now my journey begins, and I ask for Your continued guidance so that I follow Your will. I pray I'll be of use to the folks in Salt Lick Holler so this journey is fruitful. Amen.

"Perfect. This is going to be so much fun." He slapped Bryce on the back. "They even want to throw us a shindig."

"Now you *know* they haven't met us." Bryce's grin belied the words.

"They will soon enough."

❧

Hattie eyed the lopsided old ladder with misgiving. The rest of the barn had been kept up well, but the loft hadn't been used in a coon's age. She'd been working at the building steadily since they'd received Lovejoy's letter. She'd swept, scrubbed, laid fresh hay, and was running out of other things to tackle.

Today she'd moved the few critters left—the milk cow and old mule—over to the farthest stalls so they wouldn't be scared by the men moving around above. Now there was nothing to do but to ready the loft itself. Hattie had never been fond of climbing, and the way the boards for the ladder's rungs were nailed down all cockeyed didn't much help the matter.

She took in a deep breath and chided herself. *How're ya ever gonna make it to the heights of heaven iff'n yore afeared of a plain ole loft, Hattie Thales?*

With that, she twitched her skirts, steadied the ladder, and started up. Eleven rungs later, she planted her feet on the wooden floor and looked around. It was clear not a soul had been up here in years. Dirt caked the walls and the sloping roof. Moldy hay littered the floor in knee-high clumps decorated with bits of old twine.

Cleaning the barn first had been a mistake. Once she pushed this mess over the ledge, she'd have to redo most of what she thought she'd already finished. After grabbing a dusty pitchfork leaning against the far wall, she started hefting the hay. Finally about done, she heard the pitchfork thunk on something solid. Hattie cleared the rest of the gunk from around the object—a still-sturdy bench with a fair-sized trunk stuck beneath it.

Hattie glanced down before dropping the pitchfork off the loft and had to close her eyes for a moment before turning back to the matter at hand. She wrestled the trunk away from the wall and apart from the bench. It was heavier than she'd thought it would be, and she hesitated before opening it. Should she ask Miz Willow before she stuck her nose in?

She could, but that would mean an extra trip up and down the ladder. Besides, Miz Willow had already told her just to throw away anything she found up there unless it could be put to good use. Reassured, she pried open the cracked leather straps and lifted the lid. Two old blankets took up most of the room, and she pulled them out. They were clean, and once she aired them out, they'd be good to make up pallets. Beneath them she found a ball of twine and a small folding knife. She pulled out a bag and a carved wooden box, deciding not to open these without Miz Willow.

She laid the blankets on the bench, put the knife and twine in her pocket, looped the string of the bag over her wrist, and clasped the box under one arm before slowly stepping down the ladder. With her feet firmly on solid ground, she put everything down. She tossed a straw broom up into the loft, wound some of the twine around her waist to tuck in a few cleaning rags, and made her way back up the ladder.

She got to sweeping and scrubbing everything in sight, then grabbed the blankets and descended from the loft for the last time that day.

The sun was setting by the time she'd cleaned up the mess left on the barn floor and aired out the blankets. She dusted most of the dirt off her hem before going to the house. As she walked through the door, the warmth of simmering stew made her stomach growl.

"Smells good in here, Miz Willow." Hattie placed the burlap bag and wooden box she'd found on the table. This was part of the reason she loved living with the old woman—they cared for each other and shared the cooking and cleaning. Not to mention that having a healer's knowledge of yarbs made ordinary dishes full of flavor.

"Thankee kindly. Since you missed yore dinner workin' in that ole barn, I figured you could use sommat to stick to yore ribs. Got biscuits waitin' in the kettle oven, too." The widow began ladling dinner into two wooden bowls while Hattie dusted ash off the Dutch oven, lifted the lid, and took out the biscuits.

"Shore right 'bout that." She nudged Miz Willow's chair closer to the table before taking her own seat. "Would you like to pray?" Hattie bowed her head at Miz Willow's nod.

"Good Lord up above, we come to thank You for the bounty on this table and in our hearts. Thankee for my Hattie who done brought this ole woman so much joy. She and Lovejoy is like the daughters I niver had. We ask for safe travelin' for our visitors from Californy an' hope all goes accordin' to Yore will. Amen."

A comfortable silence filled the room as they ate their fill of the hearty stew and honey-drizzled biscuits. Hattie leaned back and patted her full stomach.

"That was a meal fit for a queen, Miz Willow."

"I allays was partial to possum, myself, but this were a mighty tasty squirrel in our pot tonight." The widow picked her teeth with a sharpened twig, then used it to gesture to the far end of the table. "What've you got there?"

"I don't know. They was in the trunk I found in the loft. I didn't feel right openin' 'em without yore blessing." Hattie brought over the bag and box and set them before the older woman.

"Right thoughtful of you, Hattie." She stared at the objects for a long moment before adding, "But they ain't none of mine. This was Lovejoy's house with her first husband. She invited me into her home after that husband of hers passed on." The widow's mouth puckered as it always did when she thought of Lovejoy's first husband.

Hattie didn't know much about Vern Spencer. He'd left the holler an awful lot, always coming back with things to trade—usually sugar for Lovejoy's father's still. He trapped a lot, most often coming in from the woods with a few poor critters strung up, but he must not have sold their pelts for much, because he and Lovejoy hadn't lived high on the hog. No one ever talked about it, but folks knew he'd done his wife wrong and fathered a string of babes with other women.

"Should we jist send this stuff on down to Reliable without openin' 'em?" Hattie pushed aside her curiosity.

"Seems a risky thing to do—iff'n you don't know what yore a-sendin', you'll niver know iff'n it arrived." Miz Willow leaned forward. "We could write Lovejoy an' ask her what she wants done."

"But iff'n she don' know what's in 'em, neither?" Hattie prompted, running her fingers over the carved wood.

"Reckon that might be a bother. Let's us open 'em an' then decide whether whatever it is be worth the trouble." Miz Willow reached over and undid the drawstring on the small sack. A handful of braided leather ties spilled out onto the table.

"Those'll come in right useful here'bouts." Hattie gestured toward the storeroom.

"Right you are, Hattie. Ain't nothin' important to write Lovejoy about." Her lively blue eyes fixed on the box. "That's a purty piece for shore. Cain't imagine she'd leave it behind."

"She didn't know she wasn't comin' back when she left," Hattie offered, tracing the swirling design with one forefinger. It looked to be the work of a master craftsman.

"True, but iff'n it were close to her heart, I figgur she woulda asked for it to be sent. Go on ahead an' open it, dearie." She craned her neck as Hattie flipped the latch to lift the lid.

"Mercy," Hattie breathed as a pile of golden coins came into view. She pushed the treasure trove toward the widow.

"Well, I'll be," Miz Willow declared. "Cain't think Lovejoy even knew 'bout it. She wasn't one to set on sommat as could holp others so much. You'd best fetch me pencil and paper, Hattie. This is worth more'n any letter I cain write."

Logan inched toward the door, hoping that no one would notice. His hand closed around the handle, the sliver of sunlight he exposed welcoming him outside.

"Logan!" He winced at Lovejoy's voice. "Where'd you put that sack of slippery elm I handed you?"

Wistfully he shut the door. Obviously he wasn't going anywhere, certainly not today. He cast a glance around the unusually cluttered main cabin and reassessed. If the women couldn't get everything together, he and Bryce wouldn't be leaving for Salt Lick Holler tomorrow, either.

"The brown bag about so big." Lovejoy motioned with her hands before rushing past him. "Here it is!" She snatched one of a pile of bags and waved it triumphantly.

Logan quelled the urge to groan aloud. He and Bryce

were packed and ready to go with one saddlebag apiece to hold two pairs of britches and three fresh shirts. They'd be wearing everything else they'd need, and the horses would go on a stock car. It should have been light traveling, but Lovejoy and his other softhearted sisters-in-law had other plans.

He, Bryce, Gideon, and Mike had ridden down to White's Mercantile with all the MacPherson and Chance women yesterday—and walked out with near half of it. Material, bandages, sacks, needles, knives, a teakettle, candy, leather, buckles, French-milled soap, cotton batting, wool blankets, a magnifying glass, razors and strops, fishing hooks, bandannas, brushes, hairpins, two shawls, chalk, ribbons, stockings, and pocketknives. Every bit of it was supposed to go with him and Bryce to the holler, along with the quilts and hooded cloaks the girls had all been stitching furiously since the decision had been made.

So tallied up with the wool the MacPhersons bundled up and the dried flowers and such Lovejoy measured out, two packhorses were added on to carry the gifts. The Chance men unanimously decided that the two horses wouldn't be returning, either. One would stay with Hattie and Widow Hendrick, and the other would be given to whomever Logan and Bryce deemed needed it most. The only exception was Lovejoy's father. She said, "Though I love my pa greatly, I won't be holpin' him carry his moonshine to other poor folks, and you cain bet that's jist what he'd do with the animal."

Logan pulled out his train ticket and stared, willing the date to change. No such luck. He was stuck here for another day while everybody rushed around packing. It was almost enough to make him and Bryce regret how they'd balked at the women's initial plan to just send along a list of what went to whom. Now they scurried around trundling items into packages with Delilah's fancy script designating some lucky citizen of Salt Lick Holler.

He could scarcely believe it when he thought of how he and Bryce would be hauling around more than twice as much baggage as Eunice, Lois, Tempy, and Lovejoy combined brought when they first came to Reliable. Two packhorses. He shook his head.

"Put this in that great big burlap sack for Silk Trevor's family." Miriam thrust a bundle into his arms and pointed across a veritable obstacle course.

Logan bit back a groan and trudged across the room. Tomorrow couldn't come quickly enough.

five

Logan woke up with a smile on his face. Today his journey would begin. He jumped out of bed, shaved his whiskers, and flung on his clothes in record time before realizing Bryce hadn't joined him.

"Come on. Get up!" He thwacked his brother on the shoulder with his hat. "You're the morning person, remember?"

"Nope. No recollection of that." Bryce pulled the covers over his head. "Breakfast bell ain't even rung."

"Now let me think back to what you told me when I said the very same thing the morning you decided Salt Lick Holler was the place to go. Oh, that's right. I know!" Logan yanked off the blankets and hunkered down to grin at Bryce.

"If I'd only known then how that whole thing would turn out. . ." Bryce's grumble died off as he yawned.

"That's just it," Logan retorted. "Neither of us knows how this whole thing will turn out!"

Three hours, two loaded-up packhorses, one train, and thirty-one hugs later, they were on their way. Bryce snoozed in the aisle seat while Logan kept his nose against the glass window, determined to remember every bit of Reliable so not even a twinge of homesickness would come between him and all the adventure that lay ahead.

Sure, he'd miss Gideon, Titus, Paul, Daniel, Miriam, Alisa, Delilah, Lovejoy, Obie, Hezzy, Mike, Eunice, Lois, Tempy, all the kids, and even Britches, but it would only be for a few months. Who knew what he'd see and do and who he'd meet in between. God had something for him, Logan was sure of it. And no man could regret following the road the Lord laid before him.

He took his Bible out of the pocket inside his coat, and it fell open to the story of Jacob. He read, feeling the presence of the Lord in the words, until a couple of verses stopped him cold: "So the Lord alone did lead him, and there was no strange god with him. He made him ride on the high places of the earth. . . ."

He brushed the fragile paper with his fingertips and mouthed the words. This had been Mama's Bible. His brothers had decided to use Pa's as the household Scripture and gave Ma's smaller version to Logan. They thought it was only fair, since Logan hadn't had as much time with her. Ma's faith had been a big part of her, and Logan could feel her love right along with God's whenever he opened this Bible.

He had everything he needed, and now he was heading toward whatever the Lord planned to show him.

❧

Hattie picked up the flour, salt, and water that served to make paste for the medicine labels. She combined the flour and salt but hesitated to add the water. She'd done this three times already today, and three times the paste had dried before she could put it to use. It wasn't because folks needed help. No, 'twas that they were curious and hoped to be the first to meet the men from California.

Sure enough, a knock sounded on the door. Miz Willow was off at the Peasley place helping clear up a case of poison oak. Usually that would leave Hattie alone with her thoughts and the sound of the rain. But not today. She bit back a sigh as she swung the door open.

Bethilda Cleary sailed out of the rain and into the cabin with her daughters, Lily and Lark. All three were cleaner than Hattie had ever seen them, and the girls were wearing shoes. From the looks of their tiny steps and periodic winces, the shoes were far too small.

"Good day, Mrs. Cleary." Hattie gestured for them to sit down. She'd prefer they stated their business and went along, but she couldn't let those poor girls stand in their pinched shoes for even a second. Besides, no potion Hattie could concoct would soothe the afflictions of Bethilda Cleary—two unwed daughters.

"Thankee kindly, Hattie." The woman peered into the corners of the room as though what she sought would magically appear.

"What cain I do for you and yourn?"

"Well, on account of our fine health," Bethilda's voice rose on the last two words before continuing, "we ain't had cause to visit you. So's we reckoned we should come an' see you on this. . .glorious spring day." She faltered at the end as Lark squeezed a handful of water from the sodden hood of her cloak onto Hattie's clean floor.

"I see." She didn't hide her smile. She might as well appreciate the humor in this visit, after all. "Pity yore visit hadn't waited a couple days. By then you coulda been introduced to our visitors." Hattie saw Bethilda's shoulders slump and blithely added, "We're expectin' their arrival any day now, ye ken."

"Yep. Mawma sayed as how those two rich city bachelors would be here, we'd git first dibs on account of the rain iff'n we—ow!" Lily broke off as Mama Cleary kicked her under the table.

"Well, that shore is a shame." Bethilda smiled wanly and stood up. "It'd be nice to have some new blood in these hills."

Hattie pushed back the thought of a mother mountain lion hunting for her cubs. The poor Chance brothers probably had no idea that every family with so much as one single daughter viewed them as fresh meat for the pouncing.

"You'll be shore to come on by once they get here." Hattie wasn't extending an invitation, just stating a fact.

"That's right neighborly of you. It's good to hear you won't be keeping the gentlemen all to yorself, Hattie Thales." Bethilda looked at her daughters. "Gotta give the young girls as could make 'em good wives the opportunity to meet them boys."

Hattie excused herself to the storeroom for a moment. The woman had all but accused her of having designs on the visitors and having no right to do so since she couldn't be a proper wife. As if Hattie didn't know that though she was a good woman, she wasn't a whole one. When a man took a wife, he wanted sons. Her hands fisted for a moment as she prayed for forbearance.

Good Lord up above, You know I've made my peace with the life You've seen fit to give me. I don't angle for another husband, Jesus. I'll never bear a child, but I protect the lives of all who're born into this holler. That and Yore love are more'n enough to fill my heart. Holp me to remember all the blessings You've bestowed upon me rather than my failures. The Chance brothers bring with them excitement and possibility. Please don't let me begrudge my neighbors those things. Holp me to forgive Bethilda her hurtful words and not let old sorrows taint the present. Thank You for Yore constant goodness. Amen.

At peace once again, she took a deep breath and reached for the medicine she'd come for. She took out the large jar of salve and scooped some into a smaller tin. Made with ground ivy and marshmallow root, the cream would help soothe the blisters Hattie was certain the Cleary sisters would soon be nursing. She took a deep breath, pasted a smile on her face, and went back to the table.

"It shore was nice of y'all to come and visit me. I cain't

holp but notice those fine shoes yore gals is wearin', Mrs. Cleary." Hattie waited for the older woman to nod. "But when it's wet, sometimes the leather cain rub somethin' awful. Here's a salve just in case yore gals need it."

Mrs. Cleary spoke through tight lips and gritted teeth. "That's right kind of you, but my gals are used to such things. I don't think—"

"Thankee, Miss Hattie!" Lily snagged the tin and put it in her pocket before her mother could refuse.

The glower in Bethilda's eyes warned Hattie that the woman would make her daughter sorry she'd spoken up. She thought hard for a moment before consoling her. "Well now, I ken yore right, Mrs. Cleary, but I'd shore hate to see Lily and Lark miss out on meetin' the fellas at the doin's iff'n their delicate skin should take an exception to the weather."

"Good thinkin', Hattie." Bethilda's brow unfurrowed, and she nodded sagely. "Shore am glad to have such a long-sighted healer. Sounds like the rain's lettin' up a mite, so we'll be takin' our leave."

After a flurry of good-byes and a hug from Lark, who whispered her thanks for the salve, the Cleary women set out. Hattie sank down in Miz Willow's rocking chair and buried her face in her hands. The Clearys had been her fourth visitors that day alone. What would happen once the Chance brothers actually arrived?

"We'll be pullin' in soon." Bryce, who'd somehow managed to sleep through most of the five-day trip in his thinly padded seat, tipped up his hat brim.

"Praise the Lord," Logan said fervently.

"Goin' a bit stir-crazy, are you?" Bryce grinned.

"Maybe a little," Logan admitted, "but today we saddle up and ride on to Salt Lick. I can hardly wait to get there."

"Me, too. It'll be nice to sleep lyin' down again."

"What?" Logan stared at his brother in disbelief. "You slept through the whole trip!"

"Not lyin' down." Bryce shrugged. "Besides, I think you did more dreaming than I could lay claim to."

The whistle cut off Logan's response as the train slowed on the tracks. The better part of the next hour was spent unloading everything from the train. Then came the onerous task of fitting everything onto the backs of the two pack animals. Finally, they were ready to set off.

Logan left Bryce with the horses and sauntered up to the only other fellow around.

"Excuse me, could you point us to the road to Salt Lick Holler?"

The old-timer chewed steadily on his straw before nodding and pointing. "Over yonder's the path. Ain't no road, but it'll git you and yore animules thar. 'Bout half a day's ride. We don't git many foreigners up these parts." He stared at Logan, obviously waiting for an explanation.

"Visiting some kinfolk." Logan smiled as he remembered Lovejoy's word for extended family. The man just shrugged and walked off, but it was clear the answer had been understood. Logan rejoined Bryce, and they swung up into their saddles.

Over to the west of the train tracks lay a dirt path, now overgrown from a long winter and wet spring. They set out more slowly than Logan would've liked, avoiding ruts and puddles as they followed the winding way through the mountains. Evergreens of all shapes and sizes spread thickly across the ground, punctuated by wild grass and blossoming shrubs. Squirrels and rabbits darted to safety as they rode by, chipmunks chattering at them all the while.

Occasionally they'd have to stop to clear deadwood out

of the path, fallen branches Logan remembered Lovejoy warning them about. She'd said they were called "widow makers," and one of them had caused the death of Hattie Thales's husband. With that in mind, Logan kept an eye out for dried-out trees. He didn't see many, but he did see birds flying, singing, courting, and building among the needles of practically every bough.

Overall, Logan and Bryce passed the pleasant ride in silence. It was best to take in their surroundings and enjoy the crisp fresh air for now. Besides, after five days on the train, they didn't have anything new to say to each other. That was fine. There'd be plenty to keep them busy in Salt Lick Holler.

Be polite and considerate, Logan dutifully reminded himself. *Remember that your actions reflect on Lovejoy and the Chances in general. You aren't here solely to have a good time roaming around the hills. It's not like recess at school—you're going on this trip to find what God has in store for your life. You'd better be certain you're not too busy having fun that you miss the message.*

All the same, Logan couldn't help but smile. It was going to be an eventful trip.

The sun had long since set by the time they reached the valley. They squinted to find the fork in the road Lovejoy had told them would lead to the healers' place. They inched along in deepening darkness, the only light coming from the waxing moon and more stars than Logan had ever seen before. The soft hoots of owls underscored the chirps of lovelorn crickets.

They guided their horses to the right and went a few hundred yards before spying a comparatively large structure to their left, exactly as it had been described. There. The cabin. Regardless of the weariness of cross-country travel, Logan felt a surge of excitement.

six

Hattie rolled out of bed and slipped on her overdress almost before she was awake. She grabbed her satchel and padded across the floor in her bare feet to answer the door. If someone was calling in the dark of night, it must be urgent. She opened the door to a blast of frigid night air and a man on her doorstep.

"What can I do for you?" Hattie placed her satchel between them and tried to make out who it was in the dim flicker reaching from the fireplace.

"I'm looking for the healer's home." The stranger took off his hat. "By that satchel you're holding, I'd guess I found it. You must be Miss Thales. I'm Logan Chance. I believe you're expecting me and my brother?"

"Nice to meet you, Mr. Chance." She dipped her head.

"So you two young bucks made it all right." Miz Willow hobbled up next to Hattie and squinted through the door. "Where's yore brother?"

"You must be Widow Hendrick." Logan smiled and gave a little bow. "Bryce is watching the horses. We weren't positive we were at the right place."

"You shore are. We'll have you come in and warm up after we see to yore animals. Hattie, why don't you show 'em to the barn while I brew some tea?"

Hattie fetched two lanterns and stepped outside as the first brother motioned for the second to follow. She could scarcely believe her eyes when she saw not two but four horses. Two of them were loaded down with more than she'd ever owned in her whole life. They had just enough room in the barn for the animals. Good thing she'd put fresh hay in all the stalls.

She opened the barn door and went ahead to light a few hanging lanterns so they could get the horses situated. She gestured to the wall of empty stalls.

"They can stay here. While you unload 'em, I'll fetch some water." She grabbed a bucket and went out to the well, making four trips to see to every horse's thirst.

She'd never seen the barn so full. Their mule and milk cow looked at the newcomers curiously. The chickens ignored the entire proceedings as the opposite half of the barn suddenly became occupied, and the final empty stall filled with all the gear the Chance brothers had hauled up the mountains.

"This here's the ladder to yore loft, where I've made up some pallets for you. You should be plenty warm, but if yore needin' more blankets, jist let me know straightaway." She put her hand on the ladder but didn't climb up it to show them their beds. She figured they could manage fine on their own. "Miz Willow's made you some tea inside to warm you up, iff'n you'll follow me." She blew out the hanging lanterns and left the barn.

When they reached the cabin, one of the men hurried to open the door for her. It was the first one, Logan. She'd studied their faces in the lantern light as they took care of their horses. Both had dark hair and comely features, but Logan boasted a stronger jaw and wasn't quite as tall as Bryce.

"Thankee." She acknowledged the gentlemanly gesture and walked over to where Miz Willow was rocking in her chair. The kettle steamed over the fire, while a loaf of bread warmed in the niche.

"You've both met Hattie by now, and I'm Willomena Hendrick. Most folks in these parts call me Widow Hendrick, but when folks lodge with me I prefer Miz Willow. Hattie started callin' me that, and I like it right fine. Ain't that right, Hattie?"

"True 'nough." Hattie placed a jar of blackberry preserves on the table and nodded. "I don't like bein' called Widow Thales, so I reckoned Miz Willomena probably didn't shine to it after all these years, either."

"And Willomena's a mouthful and a half, so's she shortened it to Willow." The old lady rocked contentedly.

"Because it's fittin' for a healer to be named after a soothin' yarb." Hattie finished telling the story and placed the warm sliced bread on the table along with freshly brewed tea. Then she motioned for the men to sit at the table.

"We'll be happy to call you Miz Willow. It suits you. This is Bryce, since you didn't get to meet him before we took care of the horses."

"Nice to meet you, Miz Willow. Miz Thales." Bryce took a swig of tea and raised his eyebrows. "Say, I'm more of a coffee man, but this is pretty good!"

"No arguments here. We're much obliged for your hospitality." Logan slathered his bread with jam and took a large bite.

"Yore welcome, Mr. Chance." Miz Willow beamed and rocked more quickly, the runners giving tiny squeaks on the wooden floor. "Both of you Mr. Chances."

"You can call us Logan and Bryce. Everyone in Reliable does, since there are six Chance brothers." Logan grinned. "No one'd know who you meant back home if you called any of us 'Mr. Chance.' Plenty more for the next generation, too, so we just stick to first names."

Hattie blew on her tea to avoid saying anything. These good-looking men came from a large family that was getting larger all the time. How different they would find it here, with just her and Miz Willow and no little ones to play with or cuddle.

Not that it would matter. The older youths of the holler would keep them plenty busy. Abner MacPherson and Rooster Linden would want to meet their kin. Silk Trevor's boys, Ted and Fred, would take them hunting and trapping. Asa Pleasant was teaching his Albert the best spots for fishing, and his two girls, Sky and Lizzie, were of the right age to be courted. Not to mention the Cleary gals. Hattie had a sneaking suspicion that Logan, with his bright blue eyes and easy grin, would be much in demand. Both of the handsome brothers would be before they went back home to their nieces and nephews to start having babes of their own. If any of the folks of Salt Lick Holler had their way, the mothers of those babes would be their very own daughters.

❧

When Miz Willow tried to hide a yawn, Logan knew they'd stayed and chatted long enough. He swiped one last piece of bread.

"Much as we'd like to stay right here at this comfortable table with you lovely ladies. . ." Logan glanced at Hattie when he said the words. Sweet wisps escaped the long braid down her back. They caught the red glow of the fire and framed her young face. She moved quickly and gracefully; those deep blue eyes seemed to catch every detail. He realized he'd paused too long and covered it with a yawn of his own. "It's been a long time since we hit the hay." He stood up and waited for Bryce to follow suit.

"Thanks for your warm welcome and delicious treats." Bryce rose to his feet.

"Here's a fresh lantern for you. There's another in the loft. I left water in the bucket should you wish to fill the pitcher I left on the bench up there." Hattie handed the light to him.

"Thanks. We'll do just fine. Good night."

He and Bryce made their way back to the barn and climbed the ladder to the loft. Surprised at its size, Logan held the lantern high to look around. Two pallets made of fresh hay beneath clean blankets looked homey and inviting. Several blankets piled on the end would ward away the nighttime chill. A sturdy bench held the lantern and pitcher Hattie spoke of, as well as a basin, two hand towels, and a tin cup. A large empty trunk sat in a corner where the sloping roof kissed the loft floor, and a few nails were stuck in the wall to serve as hooks. Everything was clean as a whistle.

Someone—no, not someone—Hattie had taken a lot of time to clean up this place and make it comfortable. It fit with the way she watered the horses and took care of the tea and such. Hattie Thales had a kind heart to match her pretty face.

"Nice digs." Bryce lit the other lantern and hung up his hat. He grabbed the pitcher and started down the ladder to get the water Hattie had left for them. Logan caught the bundles Bryce slung up to him. They'd want fresh clothes in the morning.

Bryce came back up to the loft and plunked down the pitcher while Logan put their clean clothes in the trunk, along with his Bible.

Then they each sunk onto a makeshift bed, pulled off their boots, and gratefully stretched out under the comforting warmth of a heap of blankets. Logan shut his eyes and immediately started to doze.

"What's going. . . You've got to be. . . Are you whistling?" Logan raised up on his elbows to peer at Bryce, who was giving a jaunty rendition of "She'll Be Comin' 'Round the Mountain."

Bryce finished the tune before answering. "Not anymore."

"Good," Logan grumbled. "Now let's get some shut-eye."

"You go on ahead. I'm not a bit sleepy."

"I'll do that. Just don't whistle anymore." Logan settled back into the warm bed and breathed deeply, waiting to drift off again.

Thrum-dum-dum-bum-thrum. The sound made Logan crack an eye open. It was too close for one of the animals to be fidgeting. "What are you doing now?"

"Hmmm. . . Oh, I guess I was tapping my fingers on the floor. Sorry." Bryce didn't sound at all repentant.

"Something on your mind?" Logan gave up trying to pretend Bryce wasn't there.

"A lot. Pretty country, ain't it?" Bryce, the most silent of all his brothers, sounded downright chatty.

"Yes, and I want to get a good night's sleep so I can explore it tomorrow." Logan yanked his blankets higher and tried to get some sleep. The sooner he fell asleep, the sooner morning would come—and with it, new faces to meet and places to explore.

"Miz Willow's a spry old gal. Did you see the twinkle in her eyes?"

"Yep." Logan thought of the wispy snatches of white hair covering the widow's head, like she was so full of energy her hair couldn't lie flat. But now wasn't the time to think about it. "Go to sleep, Bryce."

"Can't. Don't know why."

"Because you only woke up to stuff your face for the past five days." Logan glared in his brother's general direction. "If you can't sleep now, it's your own fault. As for me, I'm gonna ask you to be quiet so I can rest. There'll be a lot to do and see tomorrow."

"True. Maybe Hattie'll show us around. What did you think of her?"

Logan realized Bryce's yammering had managed to make

him too alert to sleep. He sat up and ran his hand through his hair.

"Why? You're usually the one who's more interested in animals than people." Logan was actually interested in Bryce's opinion.

"Yep. But she's kinda hard to read. She's got a servant's heart—I mean, look at how she fixed up this place for two strangers. She was awful nice about helping us in the middle of the night. I don't think they have a pump. She had to draw all that water for the horses out of a well. Reminds me of Rebekah in the Bible, but she's pretty quiet, too. I guess I'm used to hearing Miriam, Alisa, Delilah, Lovejoy, Temperance, Eunice, and Lois all gabbing to each other and directing the kids. Hattie's pretty enough. Why isn't she married?"

Logan thought it over for a while.

"She was, but he died, remember? And if she's on the quiet side, maybe it's because we met her in the middle of the night and we don't know her yet." Logan wondered what she'd be like in daylight. Would her hair still hang in a tidy braid past her waist? Would her voice still sound soft, husky, and musical?

Bryce rolled over. "She's as pretty as Eunice and Lois, and as kind as Lovejoy. I'll bet she's about as good a healer, too."

Logan thought that over. Was she smart like Tempy? He remembered the carefully slanted script and strange spelling of her letter and how she'd mentioned just learning to read and write.

"Well, I—" Logan broke off when he realized Bryce was snoring. He shook his head and lay back down. "Figures."

seven

Hattie came awake when the cock crowed, and she got out of bed straightaway.

Would the Chance brothers—*Logan and Bryce,* she reminded herself—sleep late after their journey? She'd best make enough breakfast just in case.

After slipping on her dress and rebraiding her hair, she made bread dough and left it to rise under a blue and white gingham towel. She dashed out to the smokehouse and fetched a side of bacon. Logan and Bryce looked like they could pack away a lot.

She sizzled the bacon and left it in the small oven to keep warm, then shaped the loaf and put it in the niche of the hearth wall to bake. By that time, the early dim had given way to morning's brightness, and Miz Willow had woken up.

"Why don't you go on ahead and fetch some eggs and milk whilst I put on some coffee? My old mind seems to recall one of those brothers mentioning it yester-eve."

Hattie picked up the small basket she used to gather eggs and took her time getting to the barn. She'd be as quiet as she could just in case the Chances were still asleep. Cautiously she opened the door and stepped over to the chicken coop, trying to shush the clucking birds as she searched for their brown eggs.

"Mornin'." Logan's head popped over the edge of the loft, startling her.

"Mornin'. I didn't know if y'all was awake yet." She focused her attention on shutting the coop before picking up the three-legged stool and milking pail.

" 'Course we are. We'll be down in just a minute, and I'll take care of that for you," Logan offered.

"No need." Milking cows was woman's work, but offering to help didn't make him any less of a man. She finished and stood up, leaving the pail of fresh milk on the barn floor. "Y'all cain come into the house soon as yore ready. I've got breakfast started."

"Sounds good!" She recognized Bryce's voice before she left the barn.

She gave the eggs to Miz Willow, who immediately started scrambling them once she heard that the men were on the way. Hattie strolled out to the well, pulled up the bucket, and lifted a pail of chilled milk from where they kept it hanging down by the cool water. She drew a bucket of water for the house.

By the time she poured the milk into a pitcher and put it on the table with the bacon, Logan and Bryce were knocking on the door. Real gentlemen, they were, to knock rather than just saunter in. Even though they knew they were welcome, the gesture showed good manners. Logan set down the pail of fresh milk.

"Come have a seat," Miz Willow invited, putting the eggs and coffee next to the plates and mugs.

Hattie sliced the cinnamon bread and put out some butter before joining them at the table. She sat next to Miz Willow, across from Logan.

"Would one of you gentlemen like to bless the meal?" Miz Willow invited.

"Certainly." Logan surprised Hattie by reaching across the table to take hold of her hand so they all formed a circle.

She noticed his clean hands and face, shaved jaw, and combed hair. He honored their table by coming to it as though ready for a banquet. His brother looked just as neat.

These men had more manners and common sense than most folk—and they probably suffered illness a lot less.

"Dear heavenly Father, we come before You this morning and thank You for all You've given us. We praise You for the safe journey and warm welcome we've experienced, and thank You for the hands that prepared this food. We pray for those who aren't with us now and ask You to keep them close. Amen."

Hattie smiled to thank him for his beautiful prayer. He'd blessed them as well as the food and remembered his family, too. If all the Chance brothers had been brought up as well as these—and Hattie figured they must have been—then Lovejoy was well taken care of as she deserved to be.

"Mmmm, this hits the spot." Bryce jabbed a fork into his eggs as though to punctuate the comment.

"Delicious." Logan agreed. "Thank you for getting up early to make all of this for us. Nice of you to go to the trouble." He directed this last comment to Miz Willow.

"Much obliged." Bryce reached for another slice of cinnamon bread, and Logan passed him the butter.

"Hattie do have a way 'round a fire," Miz Willow praised. "Her cinnamon bread's a favorite of ourn."

"I can see why." Logan took an appreciative bite and washed it down with some milk.

This man kept on surprising her. Most lads she knew wouldn't bother to think of how she and the widow didn't need to make so much food for just the two of them. Pa and Horace hadn't seen any need to thank her for cooking or anything else. That was her place. Not that she minded doing it, but it was nice to be appreciated for her efforts.

❧

Logan helped himself to some more bacon and passed the platter to Bryce, who did likewise. The smoky flavor of the meat was rich and filling, but he had plenty of room left over for the melt-in-your mouth flavor of Hattie's warm, buttery cinnamon bread. He was glad to see he and Bryce weren't going to strain their food supply. All the same, he'd find ways to repay them for their hospitality.

According to Lovejoy, the widow and her apprentice made a steady living. Their home featured wooden floors, two windows covered with clarified hide, a real bed, and a separate storeroom. Everywhere he looked, he saw the tiny touches of love that made this place a home.

A rag rug covered the center of the floor. Fresh flowers filled a jar on the bedside table, where a Bible held the place of prominence next to a tallow candle. Cheery curtains lined the tops of the windows, keeping out drafts and letting in some light. The bed was neatly made, and a sampler hung above it proclaiming, "A MERRY HEART DOETH GOOD LIKE A MEDICINE." He only noticed it because the same type of thing had snuck its way onto Chance Ranch with each new bride.

He wasn't able to think of anything to help Hattie and Miz Willow that Lovejoy hadn't already included in her packages. They had an outhouse and a smokehouse. The milk this morning was nice and cool, so they might have a springhouse, he figured. Then again, they might keep it dangling in a well bucket.

"I don't think they have a pump. She had to draw all that water for the horses out of a well." Bryce's observation from the night before tickled Logan's brain. Maybe he could get and install a pump. Living with Lovejoy had taught him just how much fresh water a healer could need, and the childhood memory of hauling buckets on Chance Ranch reminded him how much easier a water pump made the daily chore. The idea had merit.

"Now that yore bellies are full, I've a mind to ask you

how that Lovejoy of ourn is farin' back in Californy." Miz Willow's lively voice interrupted his thoughts.

"Just fine, ma'am." To Bryce, those three words summed it all up.

"We're awful glad to have her," Logan jumped in. "She's worked wonders with Daniel."

"No foolin'," Bryce offered. "He'd been downright surly for about three years through. Sore as a buckshot bear."

Logan shoved the coffee in front of his brother to make him stop talking. What was Bryce thinking? Didn't the alarmed look on Hattie's face clue him in? They needed to hear how well Lovejoy and the MacPherson brides were getting along.

"There's some truth in that." Logan smiled to soften the admission. "But Lovejoy came into our lives and pushed away his grief. She's a mother to Polly and Ginny Mae, and the only woman I know who could've worked her way into Daniel's heart. She's a blessing to Chance Ranch."

"Heh," the old woman said, slapping her gnarled hand upon her knee, "that's Lovejoy for shore. Has a way of cuttin' through the muck and taking care of the wounded." She gave a decisive nod. "Sounds like she's found the place God intended for her to be."

Hattie shot the old widow a questioning glance, and Miz Willow asked her next question with such cautious nonchalance that Logan could tell something was in the works.

"Don't suppose she sent a letter or word with you boys 'bout a small matter we writ to her. . ." Her voice trailed off, but her eyes flickered with surprising intensity.

"Not that I know of, but she and the others packed so much stuff for us to bring, it could be in some bundle or another." Bryce shrugged and leaned back. "We've gotta unpack it all and figure out what goes to who anyway, so we'd be glad to keep a lookout."

Miz Willow looked at them expectantly. Logan knew whatever she was expecting must be awfully important, because she stood up and rested her weight on the table.

"Well, Hattie and I've got to clear the dishes. Why don't you boys git to it. When yore done, Hattie an' I'll help you track down the folks it's intended for."

Logan reckoned that was about as close as she could politely come to a blunt, "What're you waitin' fer?" He stood up and nudged Bryce on the shoulder.

"Sounds like a good idea to me. Good way to start meeting people. C'mon, Bryce." He led the way back to the barn, where they both stared at a veritable mountain of bundles and sacks.

Each package was bound with string and adorned with a note detailing what family it was intended for. Occasionally a list of what was for whom also hung from the string. Lovejoy's neatly cramped script, Miriam's elegant letters, Alisa's grand flourishes, and Delilah's calligraphy brought back a sense of home. It seemed as though they'd packed something for every family in these parts.

Logan realized Bryce was staring at the pile with the same hopeless expression he probably wore. He could just imagine Hattie and Miz Willow coming back after they'd done all the dishes to find both of them just standing there, scratching their heads. Miz Willow just might poke them with her cane. Though twisted with age, she still held a presence that was both fun and formidable.

"Let's start laying them out so they're not just in a big heap." Logan couldn't really think of anything else to do without knowing where each family lived.

They worked for a while, finding that while some families

had one package, others had more. Logan combined these smaller individual bundles into neat piles.

I can't believe how long this is taking! We should be out of this barn by now, riding the countryside or fishing with other men of the holler. Instead, my adventure today is going to be sorting packages like a fussy old maid.

He and Bryce had just about finished laying all the things out when the women walked in.

"Howdy, Miz Willow, Miz Hattie." Logan tipped his hat. "We put yours aside over by the door.

"Thankee much, both of you. We'll git to 'em later. For now I figgur we'd best git all this organized." Miz Willow gestured expansively.

"We sure could use your help." Logan smiled. "We've already divvied it up by surname, if that's any use."

"Shore will be." Hattie nodded and stepped forward, glancing at Miz Willow. What she saw slid the small smile right off her face and made Logan realize just how tightly the older woman was clutching her cane.

"Oh, Miz Willow, I jist had a worry. What iff'n someone comes for the healer and cain't find a one of us? I'll bet Otis Nye's near run out of the devil's claw tea we give him for his rheumatiz. Why don't you go inside and brew up a batch so he cain have some straightaway iff'n he comes to call?" She gently turned the older woman to the door.

"I s'ppose you've the right of it." Miz Willow started back to the house. "Jist you let me know when yore ready. I might have some salves or poultices to send out with you." She left.

"Nice of you to find a way she could rest." Logan tried to encourage her.

"It's my fault she needs to." Hattie blinked a few times. "I forgot to make the tea to soothe her joints this mornin'. It holps with her pain and makes it so she don't swoll up so bad."

"Seems to me she's doin' just fine," Logan said, consoling her. "She can make the tea for herself now and not feel as though she's not pulling her weight. You saved her the pain of her joints and the humiliation of having to admit she needed to sit."

"I reckon." Hattie shook her head as though to clear it, making the deep red of her braid bounce along the pale yellow of her cotton dress.

Logan couldn't help but like her better for her tender heart and the way she watched over the saucy old woman. Of all the people he'd meet in the holler, he had a funny feeling he'd be glad to have met these two remarkable women first.

eight

"Wait a minute." Hattie lifted up a small parcel. "Did you two miss this?" She recognized Lovejoy's writing and smiled. "It's got yore names on't."

Bryce held out his hands, so she tossed it to him. He made short work of unwrapping two shiny harmonicas. He picked one up and handed a slip of foolscap to Logan.

"It says here you'll know who's best to teach us how to play these." Logan waved the paper. "Any ideas?"

"Yep. Li'l Nate Rucker'll learn you how. I'll introduce you later." Hattie couldn't help but grin. Li'l Nate was the burly blacksmith of the holler. It did a body good to see such a bear of a man make a sweet tune on his harmonica. "It's a good way to get to know some folk, 'specially since they're plannin' to have a sang real soon."

"A sang?" Logan repeated doubtfully.

"We have us a sang when we want to celebrate sommat. This case, yore arrival's all the reason these folks need. It'd be swell iff'n you could play a song or two by then."

Hwaaaang. Bryce gave an experimental toot. "I hope it's a ways off, in that case."

They all shared a chuckled before finishing the work at hand. It seemed as though Lovejoy, Tempy, Eunice, Lois, and the MacPherson boys had been determined to send something back for every last kinsman in the holler. She'd thought it looked like a heap of goods when the brothers first rode up, but spread out, the bundles filled the barn floor and then some. Hattie could only imagine what the packages held, but if she knew Lovejoy and those gals, everything would be useful and appreciated. The gifts would also go a fair way to making even those most distrusting of outsiders warm up to the new men.

"Seems to me we ought to see about gettin' some dinner before we load up yore horse," Hattie said. They'd decided to just start making the rounds today. Hattie thought it best for the men not to strut around with two horses packed full of goods. It might make these men seem uppity, even though she knew they weren't.

"Agreed." Bryce scrambled up the ladder.

"We'll be along soon as we're washed up." Logan shot her a grin before following.

Hattie picked up the bundles bearing her and Miz Willow's names and went into the house to wash up. Maybe she'd make some sandwiches or something that wouldn't need to cook long. Bryce hadn't left any doubt as to whether or not he was hungry.

The door was open and the window covers rolled up when Hattie came inside. She could smell the faint sulfuric tinge in the air signaling boiled eggs. Miz Willow had fixed egg salad sandwiches and sliced apples for dinner.

"You've been busy." Hattie nodded toward the table as she laid the bundles on the bed. She was glad to see Miz Willow moving around with ease. "Need me to fetch some cool water?"

"That'd be nice, dearie. I'm just going to make a few more of these here sandwiches. Those boys shore cain pack it away." Hattie heard the fondness in Miz Willow's voice and knew she enjoyed having the Chance men around. Hattie was starting to feel the same way.

She took a wooden bucket made smooth by much use and filled it with the cool mountain water. As she walked back to the cabin, Logan and Bryce joined up with her.

"I'll get that." Logan smoothly snagged the bucket without sloshing over any of the water. His thumb brushed the back of her hand, warming her.

❧

Logan clasped the handle of the bucket, feeling how warm it was from Hattie's hand. The rope was rough, a definite contrast to her soft hand.

They ate a pleasant lunch of tart apples with egg salad sandwiches on thick slices of bread. The crisply fresh water Hattie had drawn from the well washed it all down.

"We were going to bring in your packages when we came in for lunch, but Hattie beat us to it." Logan spotted them on the bed. "Maybe you ought to open 'em before we set off. There might be a note from Lovejoy that tells us something we need to know."

He couldn't dismiss the meaningful looks between Hattie and Miz Willow this morning.

"That might be a good idea," Hattie said slowly, raising her eyebrows in a silent question to the widow.

"Reckon so." With Miz Willow's nod, Hattie crossed the room and brought the parcels back to the table.

Logan made sure to move all the dishes out of the way before she got back. He and Bryce scooted as far down as they could so as not to intrude.

Miz Willow painstakingly untied the string and unfolded the neat brown paper to reveal her treasure. Although Logan could see a box and a shawl, she first picked up the note Lovejoy had written to her. She slid a wrinkled finger beneath the edge of the envelope to open it. Her mouth moved silently as she read to herself; then she put it down.

"No mention of it, Hattie. I reckon our last letter didn't make it afore these two"—she jerked a thumb at them—"took off."

Logan registered Hattie's disappointment and could hardly restrain his own curiosity.

"What were you lookin' for?" Bryce held no compunction.

Logan didn't know whether to kick him or slap him on the back for the blunt question, so he just waited for the response.

"I reckon it's up to Lovejoy to let you know. We don't have all the facts yet, but I figgur we cain tell you when yore sister-in-law gets word back to us." The widow's vague answer only raised more questions, but it would have to do. An awkward silence hung in the air.

"Fair enough. Why don't you go on and see what they sent you?" Logan ended the uncomfortable pause.

They all watched as the widow opened the pasteboard box and took out a gleaming new copper kettle.

"Ain't that a sight?" She held it up and looked at it from every angle. "I cain see ever wrinkle on my face, but it's beautiful just the same, 'cuz it's the same color as yore hair, Hattie!"

Logan privately thought Hattie's hair a much richer shade but held his peace. It wasn't the type of thing to mention.

"It'll shore come in useful for you, Miss Willow." Hattie gently took the proffered kettle and placed it in a position of prominence on one of the shelves.

Miz Willow drew out a soft-looking woolen shawl in bright purple. Hattie held it up. "Now ain't that the prettiest thing you ever clapped eyes on?" she asked before tucking it around the old woman's shoulders.

"I've been needin' a fair-weather wrap." Miz Willow stroked the fabric lovingly. "Ole one's plumb wore through."

"Don't you look a sight in yore violet shawl." Hattie stepped back to admire the color while the widow pulled out a thick hooded cloak in a deeper shade.

"Trust Lovejoy to remember my favorite color," she said with a chuckle. "Give me airs to wear the color of royalty." She handed the cloak to Hattie, who hung it on a peg near the door.

The last things in the bundle were small labeled bags Logan guessed were the healing herbs, since Hattie picked them up and carried them back to the storeroom.

Next was Hattie's turn, and she deftly untied the string to find a rose cloak identical to Miz Willow's purple one. She immediately stood up to try it on.

"Oh, it's so warm and soft!" she gasped. "I do believe they made these special for us, Miz Willow!"

Now Logan never would have thought to give any living soul anything pink, but the deep rose cloak brought a glowing blush to Hattie's cheeks. It was a good choice.

She kept it on as she unwrapped a small package of needles and a set of sharp knives. She tested the weight of each knife in her hand.

"These are wonderful. They'll shore come in handy, and this one fits my palm jist right!" Logan watched as she removed an older knife that had seen many sharpenings from the sheath around her small waist and replaced it with the new one of the same size. "Good for gathering," she explained when she noticed him looking.

"It's a good thing to have around, period." Logan suddenly realized how often Hattie must walk around alone. The healer would treat folks from all around, including men. Pretty as she was. . .well, he wasn't sorry to see her carry a knife.

❧

"Go on, off with you young'uns. I'll do the dishes and rustle up some rabbit stew and corn pone for supper. Hattie'll know when to come back." With that, Miz Willow shooed them back to the barn like they were a flock of ornery chickens.

Hattie found herself out in the barn, holding the head of one of the packhorses as Bryce and Logan lifted on all the parcels. "Shore is a fine animal—not so tall as yore ridin' horses, but sturdy strong. Glossy brown coat, too." She patted the mare's nose and gave her a carrot from the basket on the wall. Whickering, the horse tickled Hattie's palm with her soft nose, looking for more of the treat.

Blossom brayed from the stall directly opposite, and Hattie went to offer the old mule a carrot. Blossom ignored her favorite vegetable and snorted, throwing her head up.

"What's wrong, girl?" Hattie opened the gate and stroked the mule's side, but Blossom edged away. She gave a high-pitched sort of whinny and raised her left foreleg.

"Shh. . ." Hattie patted her reassuringly and bent down to see if something was caught in her hoof. It had been awhile since she'd been shod, and Hattie thought she might need reshoeing.

"She okay?" Bryce quietly stepped beside her.

"I don't see anything wrong." Hattie peered at Blossom's hoof. "I thought she might need shoeing since it was a long winter, but it seems fine."

"But she's favoring that foreleg." Something about the way Bryce said this made Hattie look at him.

"She never has before. Maybe she has a cramp." She turned back to the mule. "Guess I won't be riding you today, huh, old girl?"

"Might be worse than a cramp. She's a bit long in the tooth." Bryce walked beside Hattie and squatted for a closer look. He ran his hands expertly over the mule. "What's her name?"

"Blossom." Hattie figured she'd best get out of his way.

"Blossom here might be coming up lame." Bryce stood up and pushed back his sleeves. "I'll pack her with mud today and tomorrow put some liniment on it. Why don't you and Logan go on ahead? You can ride Blaze." He jerked a thumb at his own gray gelding, whose forehead held a white blaze.

"I don't know. . . ." Hattie wavered. Blossom was a good old friend, but her neighbors would have her hide if she didn't bring around at least one brother today. She chewed the inside of her lip in consternation.

"Bryce is about as close as you can get to a vet." Logan gently guided her toward the horse. "He has a way with animals. Besides, Blaze here's more interested in clover than running, so you don't have to worry about him being hard to handle."

"All right. To tell the truth, if I didn't show you around, I'd get in a mess of trouble with folks hereabouts." She turned to Bryce. "Before we go, is there anything I cain get to help you?"

"Nah. I know where the well is, and you've got some clean rags in the corner that'll serve. You two go on ahead without me and tell me all about it at supper."

I hope folks don't git the wrong notion with it jist bein' Logan and me ridin' alone.

nine

Logan led the packhorse; Hattie led the way. He watched her sway ahead of him, completely at ease in the saddle. The winding mountain lane gave way to a makeshift bridge over a full stream where they let the horses drink a little before continuing on their way.

"I'm leading you out to meet the Trevors. Eunice an' Lois've probably mentioned Silk to you. Jist their aunt, but reared 'em like a mother hen. The Pleasants live in the same area, so you'll meet them, too. It's fittin' that you meet up with yore kinfolk afore anyone else."

"I can hardly wait to meet them," Logan assured her. *I can hardly wait to meet everybody. I want to get to know every person in the holler—what they do, why they do it, how I can learn it. After six days of travel and a morning of unpacking, I'm finally going to have some excitement!*

"The Trevors got two twins, Ted and Fred, who're close to yore age. They're 'bout nineteen this season. You oughtta get along right well. Katherine married up with the oldest Pleasant boy, and they live here'bouts, too. Charlie'll be happy to show you the good trappin' spots." She reined in her mount.

"I ain't quite shore how to say this, but I feel you deserve a wise word or two. You know that folks up here is excited to meet you and yore brother. It's not 'cuz they'd ever in a million years thunk you brung 'em sommat, mind. But they do hold the notion they might have sommat valuable you'll take a shine to, iff'n you know what I mean." She stared at him with an undeniable intensity.

"No, not really." He hated to admit it, but he didn't have the faintest idea what she was talking about.

"Do you reckon that Eunice, Lois, and Tempy were the only unmarried women in these parts, Logan Chance?" She sighed. "Fact of the matter is, you might have a care around families with young ladies. Do you know what I mean?"

Whoa. Why didn't I see this before now? My perfect adventure has one huge hitch.

Hattie shifted in the saddle and started talking again. "You see, there ain't too many fresh faces around here, and yore two good-lookin' young bucks with a decent living and no wives attached." She looked away. "Maybe I shouldn' have mentioned it, but the cat's outta the bag now."

"Oh, no—thanks for the warning! It hadn't even crossed my mind. Now I'll know to watch my words." He waited for her to look at him again. "Hattie, I'm grateful. I'll be sure to pass this on to Bryce. See, back home it's the other way around—'bout six men to every woman. We've never exactly been in demand before." *No way she knows how truly grateful I am. The last thing on earth I hope to find in Salt Lick Holler is a bride. I need a break from children, not my own factory for 'em!*

❧

If that wasn' the most awkward conversation I've had in my whole entire life, I don't know what was. Hattie reached to pat Blaze's neck as they kept riding. *All the same, I'm glad I did. Poor guy hadn't any notion what lay ahead. He and his brother woulda been absolutely ambushed iff'n I'd hobbled my mouth.*

"Down thar's the Pleasant place." She pointed from atop the hill. "We'll go on to Silk's first and then stop by on our way back."

As they came into view of the modest cabin, Hattie thought to warn him of the dogs. "Ed Trevor breeds hound dogs. The minute you dismount, each and ev'ry blessed one of 'em'll sniff you up an' down, but they're well trained. Ed's the best breeder in the hills." As she finished, Hattie realized that the dogs weren't the only ones who'd be sniffing him over before the day was done. But he'd been warned, so she wasn't going to stew about it.

Silk Trevor came out onto the porch when they arrived, wiping her hands on a dishcloth. She waited as they tied up the horses and unloaded two packages.

"Afternoon, Hattie." Silk wrapped her in a hug and waited to be introduced to the stranger.

"Silk Trevor, this is Logan Chance." Hattie smiled as Logan held his hat to his chest.

"Nice to meet you, ma'am. Eunice and Lois tell me to give you their love." He stopped to grin mischievously. "Obie and Hezzy send their thanks. They're a happy bunch."

Silk took a deep breath as though to stop from crying. Then she changed her mind. "Aw, stuff it." She enveloped Logan in a hug.

Hattie bit back a laugh at his surprised look as Silk disengaged and held him at arm's length.

"I'm that glad to see you." She studied him head to toe. "Yore words do an aunt's tender heart some good. Why don't you two come and sit on the porch a spell? Ed and the boys'll be back afore long."

They all settled into the chairs before Silk realized they were short one brother. "Weren't there supposed to be two of you Chance men?" she asked as she started to rock.

"Yes, ma'am," Logan agreed, only to be cut off.

"Oh, you cain call me Silk."

"That's nice of you, Silk. I go by Logan, just so you know." His friendly invitation earned a nod from Silk.

"Bryce came with me, but he's down at Miz Willow's place right now."

"That's right," Hattie explained. "He thinks Blossom might be coming up lame."

"That's a sorry shame, Hattie. Blossom's been 'round long as I cain remember. Maybe there's sommat cain be done."

"If there is, Bryce'll know it. He has a way with animals," Logan said, repeating what he'd told Hattie earlier.

"Just like our Hattie has a way with holpin' people." Silk's compliment made Hattie's cheeks go hot, so she ducked her head for a minute.

"I believe you're right," Logan said. Hattie could feel Logan looking at her, so she reached down and picked up the package labeled "Silk."

She passed it to Logan, since it had been placed in his trust. Besides, she had no business giving the gifts of others.

"Right." Logan bent to pick up the one marked "Trevor Men" and held them both toward Silk. "These are from Eunice, Lois, and their husbands, I believe."

"Thankee for bringin' 'em." Silk put a hand over her eyes and looked out into the distance. "I think I see Ed and the boys, so how 'bout we wait a minute?"

In no time at all, Silk was introducing Logan to her husband and sons. "This is Ed, and these are our boys, Ted and Fred. Meet Logan Chance from Californy."

They all shook hands before taking a seat, the twins hanging a brace of rabbits from the roof.

"Nice place you got here," Logan praised. "Good land."

"Thankee." Ed beamed at him. "Hear tell you Chances don't do too bad yoreself." He cast a look around. "Say. . ."

"Bryce is at Miz Willow's, tending to her mule. I'll bring him up this way later in the week," Logan promised.

"Yore welcome anytime, anytime." Ed put his pipe between his teeth. "Me an' m' boys was just emptyin' our traps." He glanced proudly toward the rabbits.

"We'd be happy to show you an' yore brother around," Ted offered eagerly.

"I'd like that." Logan nodded. "Hattie tells me you know the best hunting and trapping spots in the hills."

"Shore do." Fred puffed out his chest. "Why don't you both come 'round early tomorra an' we'll go lookin' for deer?"

Hattie gave a slight shake of the head, hoping Logan would pick up on the signal. There were plenty more folks she needed to take Logan and Bryce to see afore they went off gallivantin'.

"Nice offer, but since we just got here, I think we still have a lot of people to meet." Logan leaned forward. "Can we take you up on it a bit later? We'll be here through summer."

"Like I said"—Ed blew a ring of smoke in the air—"anytime."

❧

Logan rubbed the grit from his eyes and flexed his feet. After meeting the Trevors and Pleasants, they'd set off for home at dusk. Once they'd shared a hearty dinner, he and Bryce had groomed all the horses and given them a good rubdown. Now he and his brother sat in the loft, winding down but not ready to sleep.

"How's Blossom going to fare?" At dinner, Logan had heard Bryce assure the women that their mule was feeling better and would be even more improved the next day. But that only meant the animal wouldn't be in pain—not that she'd be able to work.

"Better. We'll see how it goes after the liniment, but she wasn't suffering from cramps." Bryce shook his head. "The old girl's coming up lame in that foreleg, if I'm not mistaken."

"You rarely are." Logan paused before giving voice to his next thought. "We intended to leave behind the packhorses. I can't think of anyone I'd rather give one to than Miz Willow and Hattie."

"Yep." Bryce settled the matter with one word. "Speaking of which, tell me more about the folks you met today."

"Good people, every one. They aren't well-to-do by any stretch of the imagination, but they're willing to share what they have." Logan leaned back and rested his head against his hands.

"I believe it. Sounds like you're describing Hattie and Miz Willow." Bryce lay back. "Fits in with Lovejoy's ways, too."

"Silk Trevor's a warm soul. She's the one who reared Eunice and Lois. Looks like them, only softer around the eyes with age."

"Sounds 'bout right, since she's their aunt." Bryce nodded.

"Her husband, Ed, is a straightforward man. Raises hound dogs. Takes care of his family best he can. Smokes a pipe." Logan remembered the perfect rings of smoke. "Their two sons are twins, Ted and Fred. Both are blond and freckled, and I can't tell 'em apart. Offered to take us hunting and trapping once we've met everybody in the holler. They're probably a year or two younger than I am."

"Good. I'd like to explore the land a bit, stretch my legs." Bryce rolled over onto his side. "It'd be good to bring back some game to replenish Miz Willow's smokehouse."

"Just what I was thinking," Logan agreed. "Their daughter Katherine married the oldest Pleasant boy. He might come along when we go hunting, might not. His wife's expectin' again. It's her third. Hattie went inside with her to check up on everything. She's doing just fine."

"If she's anything like Eunice and Lois, she'll barrel through it like a champ." Bryce grinned. "Reckon Lois might've delivered by now. When we left, she looked liable to pop at any minute."

"Could be. Lovejoy will write when it happens." Logan worked a crick in his neck. "Last stop today was the Pleasant place."

"Sounds nice," Bryce mused. "The Pleasant place. Could be a fancy hotel."

"Not by a long shot. It's a cabin smaller than Miz Willow's and not as well built. Asa and his wife, Mary, still have three children home. His son wants to take us fishing." Logan looked forward to the shade and clear mountain stream. Fresh fish was one of his favorites.

"I'm up for it. Will the other two kids come along?"

"Sky and Lizzie are young ladies, Bryce." Now came the time to tell Bryce about Hattie's warning. "Actually, there's something Hattie mentioned I need to pass on."

"Yeah?" Bryce sat up.

"Before we visited that family, she gave me notice that there's more than one family around here with unmarried young ladies."

"Well, that's to be expected," Bryce said with a snort.

"I guess. I just never thought about it," Logan admitted. "Truth is, Hattie said they don't get a lot of visitors up this way."

"Coulda told you that by the almost-empty train." Bryce lay back down. "That's what makes it an adventure."

"Still, she was saying they don't meet new men very often, especially well-established bachelors."

"Stands to reason."

Logan could tell the exact moment Bryce got it, because he shot up like his pallet was covered in fire ants.

"You mean they'll be makin' eyes at *us*?" Alarm and disbelief painted Bryce's question.

"Yep." Logan made use of Bryce's favorite answer.

"Did Hattie tell us what to do about it?" Bryce did his best to pace around the loft, without much luck.

"Just watch what we say so we don't put any ideas into their heads."

"Sounds to me like they had ideas before we even got

here!" Bryce walked into the bench, banging his shin and sloshing water onto the floor. He sank back down onto his pallet and used one of the hand towels to mop up the spill.

"Take it easy. Hattie just thought we deserved advance notice. Don't spend time alone with any of 'em, is all." Logan blew out the lantern and pulled up the covers.

Bryce groaned. "Sounds to me like this is gonna be more of an adventure than we reckoned."

"I'll watch your back," Logan bargained. "You watch mine."

ten

After serving up and polishing off a breakfast of flapjacks and sausage, Hattie began clearing the dishes.

"Bryce and I'll go muck out the barn and load up Legs." Logan handed her his plate.

"Sounds fine." Hattie added the plate to the pile as the men took their leave.

"Did he just call one of those packhorses Legs?" Miz Willow started wiping off the table.

"Yep." Hattie smiled. "His legs look too long for his body, and when he's loaded up, they say that's pert near all you cain see of him."

"Probably should've made him a racehorse," Miz Willow suggested.

"Too broad in the shoulders and flanks to summon enough speed. Bryce said it's kinder to give him work he cain accomplish and be valued for." Hattie went outside to wash the dirty dishes.

Lord, in a funny way I'm sorta like Legs—at first glance, it seems like I was meant to be a wife and mother, but the fact is I weren't made for it. Instead, You've given me a purpose and work I cain accomplish. I know I come up short, but in Yore arms I cain reach out to holp others. I thank You for that, Jesus. Let me not lose sight of the blessings You've given me.

She finished the dishes with a light heart, humming under her breath. Then she went inside to put them away.

"Is there anything I should be on the lookout for as we ride today, Miz Willow?" Sometimes the widow knew odd spots where valuable yarbs grew. Hattie hadn't managed to memorize them all just yet, but she was working on it.

"Not today, Hattie. I figgur you'll have yore hands full enough. Now I've packed some salted meat, biscuits, and apples in that thar saddlebag for dinner, though I've a notion you might be invited somewhere. Not good to rely on such things, though, so thar's plenty for all three of you." Miz Willow kissed her on the cheek. "I'll be seein' you afore supper, I reckon."

"Depends. We're going to visit Rooster, and I'll have a look-in on Abigail Rucker, since her husband's on a trip to Hawk's Fall this week." Hattie paused. "But we pass the Cleary place, so if they git a-holt of us, it'll take forever."

"I suppose. Jist do yore best to be gone in a trice." Miz Willow grimaced. "Iff'n that don't warsh, jist don' let Bethilda corner 'em."

"I cain't make any promises."

❧

Logan finished mucking out the last stall, then walked over to find Bryce hunched over, rubbing Dr. J. H. McLean's Volcanic Liniment on Blossom's ailing leg.

"How's she comin' along this morning?"

"Hard to say." Bryce frowned in concentration. "She doesn't shy away when I touch her, but she still stays off it."

"Any chance of improvement?" Logan pressed.

"A little. She'll probably be able to use the leg a bit, but she'll favor it a good long while. If it's a bone split, she won't ever carry weight again." Bryce stood up and rubbed his hands on a rag. "Fact is, she's old, Logan. Too old to work."

"You've done what you can. We'll see to it that Hattie and Miz Willow are provided for." Logan lifted a saddle off the stand. "C'mon and help me saddle the horses—Hattie's taken a liking to Legs, so we'll load up the other one."

"She can ride Blaze again."

Something about Bryce's too-casual air made Logan turn around. "You'll have need of Blaze today," Logan stated matter-of-factly.

"I was thinking. . ." Bryce edged back toward Blossom's stall, and Logan knew what was coming.

"Oh, no you don't." He pinned his brother with his best glare. "No way you're hiding out in this barn and leaving me to meet everybody on my own."

"If there's a need, it'll be accepted." Bryce looked at something beyond Logan's shoulder rather than meet his brother's gaze.

"There's not. Yesterday you were needed. Today Blossom won't need liniment again until this evening. You're coming." He punctuated the order by hefting Bryce's saddle at him. "No brother of mine's gonna turn tail over meeting a few gals. Get going."

"Fine." Bryce straightened his shoulders. "I'll go. But I ain't talking to a one of 'em."

"Deal." From what Logan had seen, he wouldn't have to. Folks 'round Salt Lick Holler were anything but shy. They saddled all the animals and were finishing loading the packhorse when Hattie showed up.

"Are y'all ready?"

"You bet. We've loaded up everything for Abner, Rooster, Goody, and Nessie." Logan gestured to the packhorse.

"Blossom's leg is covered with some liniment, so we saddled up Legs for you." Bryce led the horse around. Hattie rested her medicine satchel on the pommel and swung up.

"Thankee." She stroked Legs's mane and crooned at him for a minute. "We get along just fine."

Logan rode alongside her while Bryce led the packhorse and brought up the rear. They went the opposite direction from the path they'd taken yesterday. The road wound uphill. The higher they climbed, the more trees crowded along the path, so full of birds it seemed as though the plants themselves sang to them.

"We'll be passin' the Cleary place. I reckon it's jist early enough not to bother them." Hattie's tone took on an unfamiliar flat note. "We'll probably be seein' 'em on the way back."

Logan turned around to make sure Bryce had heard the message; Bryce nodded. They saw a ramshackle old cabin, the wood bleached white by sun and rain, sitting in a clearing peeking through the trees. He figured that must be the Cleary place and noticed how Hattie picked up the pace as they passed it.

They reached the stream he remembered crossing the afternoon before and figured it must wind through the hills. Since there was no bridge, Hattie led them to a shallow embankment, and they crossed through the water. Legs carried Hattie across, and Logan and Bryce made it through with damp boots as they coaxed the packhorse across.

"It's jist past this turn," Hattie told them as they let the horses have a drink. "Don't quite know how to say this. . ."

"It's all right." Bryce grimaced. "Logan already told me how it is."

Logan watched Hattie's cheeks turn bright pink. It must be something different.

"What is it, Hattie?" Something about Lovejoy's dad tickled the back of his mind.

"I don't know if Lovejoy told you." She hesitated, and her voice dropped. "Mr. Linden owns a still."

"Yeah." Bryce nodded. "I remember Lovejoy sayin' her pa made moonshine."

"Well, Rooster says he takes pride in his work, so he keeps

a close eye on the. . ." She searched for words. "The quality of his product."

"Samples his own wares, eh?" Logan said.

Hattie nodded sadly. "Folks call him Rooster. Used to be he'd jist git jolly, but of late, he's taken a different turn." She jutted her chin toward the curve in the road. "I'm not shore what mood he'll be in."

Logan could feel his own frown. What Hattie was trying so hard to state delicately was that the man had become a mean drunk, and she'd been around him enough to know it wasn't an occasional occurrence.

"Is 'Rooster' his real name, or do folks just call him that because he gets roostered?" Bryce's voice made him pay attention again.

"You know, we've all called him Rooster for so long I cain't remember iff'n he has a proper name." Hattie shrugged. "Since Nessie's fella up and ran off, she's done her best to take care of her pa. Goody pitches in now and then, too."

Nessie and Goody were, if Logan remembered right, short for Gentleness and Goodness. Ma Linden had named her girls for the fruit of the Spirit in an effort to raise them well in spite of her husband's dubious occupation. Lovejoy was firstborn, Peace had died young, and Kindness was stillborn. Temperance was Micah MacPherson's Tempy, and these were the other two of the sisters. Lovejoy must not have known about Nessie's husband running off, or she would have mentioned it. She wasn't the type of woman who'd leave one of her sisters alone to fend for herself with an angry drunk for a father.

"I see." Logan met Hattie's gaze to let her know he fully understood the problem.

"Sorry to hear that." Bryce shook his head. "Glad to know in advance, though."

Hattie just nodded and got back in the saddle. Logan felt the blood pumping in his veins, and his eyes narrowed. Whatever was to come, he'd be ready for it.

I wonder what we'll find once we round the corner.

"Hattie, I'll take the lead now."

❧

Hattie pretended not to hear Logan. Instead, she nudged Legs to go a bit faster so the brothers were a few paces behind.

"Hello!" she called loudly so Rooster wouldn't think they'd snuck up on him. "Nessie, Rooster! It's Hattie Thales, and I brung you some visitors!" Best to warn him so he didn't think he had a pair of trespassers on his land. When Rooster was soused, it wasn't completely out of the question that he'd answer company with a shotgun—especially if they were strangers.

Logan pulled up beside her and shot her a dark glower before he scanned the area. "Don't try that again."

She smiled at him innocently. If he didn't like her precautions, well, he'd have to live with them.

Nessie came out of the house to greet them. Bryce busied himself tying the reins to a tree while she spoke.

"Howdy, Hattie. Mister. Mister." She cast a nervous glance toward the barn. "What cain I do for you folks?"

"Mornin', Nessie." Hattie patted the girl's arm to reassure her. "These are Logan and Bryce Chance, Lovejoy's kin. We come to visit you and yore pa, iff'n he's feelin' up to it."

"I reckon it's a good day for a visit." Nessie gave a slow nod. "Why don't you wait in the shade whilest I fetch 'im from the barn."

"Shore thing."

They waited as Nessie hurried to the barn. When she opened the door, a string of curses fouled the air before she swung it shut again.

"If she says it's a good day for a visit, then he ain't riled. He'll put on his manners for yore company." Hattie caught Logan and Bryce sharing a meaningful glance, and she gave a tight smile.

At least they'd taken her words to heart. Facing a man in the grip of drink was a bitter thing. No less taxing than telling his daughter in Californy that her old man had taken a bad turn. She and Miz Willow hadn't managed to work up the nerve yet, for fear Lovejoy would fret over things she couldn't change. Now maybe Logan and Bryce could help do something about the situation. Maybe not.

Rooster burst out of the barn, slapping his hat on his head and stumbling a little to meet them. Nessie carefully shut the barn door behind her and followed at a little distance, wringing her hands.

"Howdy." Rooster vigorously pumped Logan's hand. "Niiish ta meetcha." He turned to Bryce and did the same. "You, too."

He stood back to get a good gander at them, puffing out his gray-streaked red beard and putting his hands on his suspenders.

"Which one of you whippersnappers married m' girl?"

eleven

The man reeked of whiskey and all but fell over when he leaned back to look at them. Logan and Bryce exchanged another look, neither one too eager to answer their brother's father-in-law.

"Pa," Nessie spoke in a low whisper. "Neither of them—"

"What?" Rooster reared back and reeled forward. "Which one of you low-down polecats be livin' with my Lovejoy in sin? Come on, take it like a man." He brandished unsteady fists and danced around—the better to roar at each of them.

Logan had seen about enough. On a handful of occasions, he'd taken a nip of the hard stuff and knew how it could change a man. Since he'd gotten right with the Lord, he'd laid off the stuff. This man needed to have his head dunked in a trough a few times, followed by a pot of strong coffee and a long talk with a brother in Christ.

For now, there'd be no reasoning with him. Logan started to roll up his sleeves and saw Bryce do the same. The water trough stood about twenty paces to their left. He only hoped the thing was full of enough water to cool Rooster's hot head.

"Now then, Rooster." Hattie stepped in front of Logan. "Jist calm down a minute."

"Calm down! These heathens done ruint my firstborn!"

Logan put his hands on Hattie's upper arms and made to sweep her behind himself. She didn't budge, so he tried to step around her. Then she moved—back in front of him. He gritted his teeth as she kept talking.

"No, Lovejoy married *Daniel* Chance. These are Logan and Bryce, come to tell you what a good wife yore daughter is to their brother."

It took two repetitions before understanding banked the fire in the old man's eyes. He swiped off his hat and scratched his head. "I've made a right ole mess of things, ain't I?"

"You've raised fine daughters, Mr. Linden." Logan finally succeeded in gently pushing Hattie behind him. "But your actions aren't doing them proud."

"Oo-ee." Rooster sucked in a shallow breath. "That do cut to the quick." He hung his head. "You don' need to tell anybody 'bout my lack of manners. I'd hate to shame Lovejoy. Schhee's been good to me." He slung his arm around Nessie, who had to take a step forward so as not to buckle. "We miss her 'round here."

"I'm sure you do, Mr. Linden," Bryce acknowledged, "but that's no reason to ply yourself with liquor."

"Here now." Rooster drew himself up. "Don't be castin' as–asp–aspursi, uh, sschoe black on m' good name."

"He jist tole it like he sees it, Rooster." Hattie came forward again, and Logan didn't try to stop her. The old man's humiliation had sobered him up a bit. " 'Tis barely even noon." Her voice lowered to such a soft whisper that Logan had to strain to catch it. "Miz Willow's been wantin' to speak with you about it for a long while now."

"Did yer brung me shum of my headache tonic?" Rooster shrank into himself, looking thin and frail. "I've need for more."

"No, Rooster." Hattie patted his shoulder. "You need to come down to the cabin so we cain talk 'bout what's best to cure them headaches."

"I been doin' tolerable." Rooster jerked a thumb at his daughter. "Nessie here'll go on down for some more tea."

"No, Pa." Nessie's small voice hung in the wind.

"We're happy to see Nessie anytime. Like Logan said, you've raised fine gals, Rooster," Hattie soothed. "But Miz Willow and I cain't be givin' you yore medicine when you don't come in. As healers, we need to make shore we're a-givin' you the right treatment. Why don't you come on down, and we'll talk about it?"

Logan realized what she was trying to do. She and Miz Willow planned to confront the man about being jug-bit, but Rooster avoided them. Now Hattie wouldn't treat his ale head until they'd discussed the real problem. Logan only hoped that when the man came to the healer, he'd be in such bad shape he'd agree to almost anything. He'd seen men who had to hit rock bottom before drying out and staying sober. He was only glad the Lord had spared him from being one of them.

One thing's for certain: I'll be there when Rooster Linden comes to call. The man's a threat. Poor Nessie looks worn down. Under no circumstances will I allow Rooster to be alone with Hattie or Miz Willow.

❧

By the time Rooster had settled down and agreed to stop by and have a long-overdue chat with Miz Willow, the sun shone high in the sky. Hattie took Nessie aside for a little chat after Bryce handed her a parcel. They went and sat at the base of an old elm while the men talked and Rooster opened his package.

"I've not seen you in a while, Nessie." Hattie kept her voice light. "How are you getting along?"

"Fair to middlin', I suppose." Nessie toyed with the end of her string. "You know how it goes."

"Nessie." Hattie waited until she looked up. Hard to believe Nessie was two years younger—life had her looking careworn as an old quilt. "I do know. That's why I ask."

"Oh." A tear slid along the side of Nessie's nose. "Pa's never clear these days. Usually he's jist melancholy and sits alone jawin' at himself, and some days he's right cheery and gits out his jug to play awhile. Then he's pert near tolerable. But when he's riled. . ." The floodgates opened. "I know he don't mean the things he says, but a girl cain only hear it so many times afore it seems true. I jist stay outta his way as best I cain and make shore there's sommat for him to eat iff'n he wants it. Thar's nothin' else I cain do to holp him. I jist hafta watch him drink hisself into an early grave."

"Here you go, honey." Hattie put her arm around the gal's shoulders and handed her a clean hanky. A healer was never without a few clean cloths. She waited for Nessie to cry herself out a bit.

"I mean, he only hit me that once, and it were an accident 'cuz I was a-pullin' him away from the fire and his arms was flailin'. So don' worry yerself 'bout that a-tall. He really ain't a violent man." Having said her piece, Nessie stopped talking.

"Why don't we put it afore the Lord, Nessie?" It was the best advice Hattie had. "I'll pray with you for yore pa, iff'n you want."

"Thankee, Hattie." Nessie twisted the handkerchief a few times before letting it drop in her lap.

Hattie took Nessie's hands in hers and gave a reassuring squeeze. She could only hope that she and Miz Willow were successful in talking turkey with old Rooster when he finally came to call. If he didn't want to change, there was precious little they could do about it except pray.

"Dear heavenly Father, we come to You now in search of Yore guidance. We know You call Yore children to walk 'with longsuffering, forbearing one another in love,' and we ask for Yore holp in putting that into practice. Nessie's pa is in a bad way, Lord. He dug hisself a hole so deep that his daughter cain't hardly look after him and see the light herself. We know of Yore words on those who abuse likker: 'Woe unto them that rise up early in the morning, that they may follow strong drink; that continue until night, till wine inflame them!' Well, Father, I reckon Rooster's feeling that woe, and we pray it brings him back to Yore love. Let Yore glory inflame his heart and displace the cheap lures of moonshine. Amen."

Nessie gave her a watery smile and leaned back to dry her eyes. The both sat in silence for a minute, and Hattie was grateful for the time they had alone. The men never need know how much Nessie needed support.

"Thankee. I don't know what I'd do without you, Hattie Thales. I think the Lord gave this holler a great blessing when He called you to be a healer. There's wounds as cain't be seen by most, but you've the gift of carin'. You remind me how the Lord is always with us." Nessie reached out to stop Hattie from smoothing her braid. "Now don't be fiddlin'. I know yore modest, but it does no justice to you nor gives glory to the Lord to dismiss earned praise. It's honest appreciation, Hattie." Nessie's eyes grew moist again, and her voice dropped to a whisper. "It's all I have to give you."

"Don't you start up again." Hattie shook a finger at her before enveloping her in a hug. "Else you'll git me goin', too." She pulled back and smiled. "Besides, we have this here parcel from yore sister to open." She tapped the package. "Why don't you have a look?"

Nessie carefully untied the string and pushed back the blue calico fabric as though it were made of gold. She had to unwind it a few times before she was finished.

"It's so beautiful. There's enough here to make me a new dress." Nessie stroked a length of the material before picking up the note inside. "Lovejoy knows I cain't read, so I s'pose she reckoned on me gittin' some holp. How've yore letters been comin' along, Hattie?"

"Just fine. I'd be tickled to read it to you." Hattie accepted the envelope and read Nessie the entire letter; Lovejoy wrote that she missed her and hoped she was well, that she was doing fine and so were Daniel, Polly, Ginny Mae, and all the others. She said she hoped the things she sent would come in useful and finished off by giving her love and prayers.

"It does my heart good to hear from her." Nessie smiled and returned her attention to the package lying open on her lap. She pulled out a pack of needles, a pair of ribbons the same shade of blue as the calico, and a fawn-colored hooded cloak just like Hattie's rose one, Miz Willow's purple one, and Silk's buttercup yellow one. When she unfolded the cloak, she found French-milled soap, two pairs of stockings, and a new hairbrush, exactly like the other three had. They'd just not held them up in front of the menfolk.

"Mercy. Lovejoy weren't foolin' when she said she's livin' fine." Nessie couldn't stop smiling as she refolded the package. "There's not a thing here I cain't use—and so many luxuries, I'll feel like a queen." She stood up. " 'Tween yore prayer and Lovejoy's package, I feel so loved and blessed, I cain hardly stand it."

"S'pose we ought to join the menfolk. I've still got to check on Abigail Rucker this afternoon." Hattie stopped to give Nessie one last hug. "Remember how yore feeling now and know yore never without holp. The Lord takes care of His own."

twelve

Hattie heard the cock crow and snuggled under the covers for a mite longer. Logan and Bryce had gone off to Hawk's Fall to visit Abner MacPherson, whose three boys had married Tempy, Eunice, and Lois. They'd set out yesterday morning and wouldn't be back until tomorrow night—just in time for church on Sunday.

She and Miz Willow were happy with some boiled oats and brown sugar, so she could afford to snuggle in for a little bit this morning. When the flames in the hearth began to gutter, she got up to lay on some more wood. No matter what the season, evening through morning in the mountains could put a chill in a body. She slipped into her clothes and set water to boil for the oatmeal before she went to milk the cow and bring in fresh cream to add to their breakfast.

"Mornin'." Miz Willow was up and stirring the oats when she got back in, her pretty new shawl wrapped around her shoulders.

"Mornin'." Hattie nodded toward the pot. "Have I got time for a quick barn muckin' afore it's ready?" In addition to their milk cow and Blossom, who was on the mend, they still housed the two packhorses Bryce and Logan had left behind since they'd only had one or two packets for Abner.

"I reckon you'll be done by the time it's cool."

Hattie went back to the barn and got straight to work. After breakfast, she and the widow planned to do the wash while the brothers weren't around. Miz Willow had told the men to leave out anything they needed cleaned before they left, and Hattie found a neat bundle of shirts and britches in the barn.

She finished lickety-split and went back to the bowl of creamed oats and brown sugar Miz Willow had already served up for her. It was perfect with cool milk. The widow favored hers with tart cranberries; she said it woke her up. Hattie remembered her mama saying each bowl of oatmeal was special to the person who ate it.

I wonder why Lovejoy warned us that Logan hates oatmeal. It's one of my favorites. There's so much you cain do with it—add honey, raisins, preserves, cinnamon, maple syrup, berries. . . . Oh well. I'll jist enjoy it today and tomorra, seein' as how we won't make it for what's left of spring—or most of the summer.

After breakfast, she started heating water and hauling it to the washtub outside while Miz Willow cleaned the dishes. Soon enough, the scent of strong lye tinged the mountain air as Hattie put the washboard to work. Then she let the clothes soak in the washer before rinsing them in clean water. It took all morning to finish the clothes.

"I figgur we'd best stop for some dinner." Hattie hung the last few items on the clothesline with the clothespins Asa Pleasant had fashioned for them. It would do Miz Willow good to sit a spell before they tackled the towels, sheets, and rags. Everything in the healers' house had to be kept clean as a whistle.

"Sounds good to me."

They retrieved some salted fish from the smokehouse and used the last of the bread they'd baked the day before, washing it all down with lots of water.

"Warshin's a thirst work." Miz Willow poured her another cupful of water. "Always seems like the smell of the lye gets caught in yore throat."

"But it feels powerful nice to sleep on fresh sheets and put on a crisp, clean dress." Hattie wiped off the table and set more water on to boil.

She was bringing out a kettleful of piping hot water when she saw the Clearys opening Miz Willow's garden gate. "Seems we have us some visitors," she muttered to Miz Willow, who straightened up as best she could.

"Good afternoon, Bethilda."

"Afternoon, Miz Willow. Hattie." She sailed toward them across the yard, Lily and Lark in tow.

Hattie could see the tight lines around Bethilda's mouth. Suddenly, working over a vat of hot lye water seemed like a fine way to spend the afternoon. She took a deep breath and pasted on a smile. "What seems to be the trouble?" Hattie knew the problem wouldn't be medicinal.

"Silly girl." Bethilda gave a forced laugh. "This be a social call."

"Well, in that case I s'pose we'd best set in the shade awhile. I cain make us some tea." Miz Willow ushered them to the porch, but Bethilda followed her inside.

"We went to visit Abigail Rucker t'other day." Bethilda sat down at the table, and her daughters followed suit. "Bless her heart, poor thing's bigger'n a bear. She mentioned as how Hattie'd been to see her jist the day afore, and how nice it'd been for Hattie's visitors to wait outside like gentlemen while they talked 'bout the babe to come."

Hattie closed her eyes for a moment. Bethilda Cleary knew she'd been up her way and hadn't stopped by to introduce the Chance brothers. Hattie reached for the chamomile—anything soothing couldn't hurt. Upset, Bethilda Cleary resembled a riled polecat—the stink she raised would cover everyone around.

"And I asked myself, how was it we hadn't seen you or yore new friends?" Bethilda's tone sounded sticky as honey but held none of the natural goodness.

"To tell the truth, Bethilda, we counted on stoppin' by but owed it to Rooster and Nessie to see them first, seein' as how he's their brother's father-in-law." Hattie saw Miz Willow nodding in support. "Took a mite longer'n we reckoned, and it were dark when I'd finished lookin' in on Abigail." She wouldn't mention how she'd taken Logan and Bryce through the meadow instead. "We wouldn't want to impose on you—and with no warning whatsoever!"

"I'm shore I done made it clear as a mountain stream that we was anxious to meet the bachelors." Bethilda's eyes narrowed. "Lily and Lark are bound to get along with 'em like peas and carrots. That bein' the case, I've got to ask why yore keepin' 'em away."

"Fiddlesticks, Bethilda Cleary," Miz Willow broke in. "You know better. Hattie cain't control the sun, and happens right now, the boys went to Hawk's Fall."

"Aw," Lily groaned, "you didn't scare them off, did yer, Hattie?"

"We was itchin' to meet 'em." Lark sounded downright mournful.

"They went to visit Abner MacPherson and take him word from his sons back in Californy." Hattie poured the tea into five cups. "That's all."

"I heard they brung more'n words." Bethilda peered around. "Caught wind that Lovejoy and the MacPhersons done sent gifts to everybody in the holler."

"They brought things for kin and such," Hattie clarified. Clearer than a cloudless night, the Cleary's were hopin' for something from Californy in addition to husbands.

"Oh?" Bethilda glanced slyly at the two cloaks hanging by the door before nodding at the copper teakettle. "Didn't realize you was kin."

"Lovejoy an' Hattie is kindred spirits. All healers are.

'Sides, Hattie's the one what's takin' care of her brothers."

"I see." Bethilda stood up. "Well, you'll be shore and let us know when they're back from Hawk's Fall. We wouldn't want Hattie to take all that *carin'* on herself."

Hattie bit her lip as the Clearys left, tamping down a surge of anger at Bethilda's implications. She emptied the teakettle and went outside to rinse the cups clean. Miz Willow followed her.

"Don't you let Bethilda Cleary direct her pointed words and pierce yore heart, Hattie. It reflects on her, not on you." Miz Willow waited until she nodded in response. "Now let's finish up this warshing. Bethilda's visit set us back."

"Shore did."

Logan and Bryce arrived at Hawk's Fall after dark and made their way to the MacPherson farm. Abner ushered them to the barn, where they saw to the horses, then bedded down in the loft.

Logan could scarcely believe this was the selfsame loft shared by Obadiah, Hezekiah, and Micah McPherson before they came out to California. He and Bryce barely fit in the space when they lay down. How three grown men had slept here was beyond him. Especially since Obie and Hezzy were absolutely mammoth. Logan now knew they'd gotten their height and girth from their father. It seemed as though Micah had inherited his mama's stature and his pa's smarts.

They got to know Abner better the next day when he showed them around. "You already seen the barn. Ain't as grand as the Peasleys' up yonder—they breed mules—but it serves." Abner puffed out his chest with pride. "M' boys set up in Californy and then sent me money for a new one."

"Sturdy animal." Bryce praised a nearby mule. "I'll bet he's good at pulling a plow."

"Right you are." Abner took them out to a shed behind the barn. "This here's the fancy plow m' boys wanted me to have." He took off his hat. "The Lord blessed us with fine sons. We raised 'em right in the sight of God, and now they share their blessings. Look 'round. We'll have us a bumper crop this year."

"Good to hear," Logan affirmed. "Obie, Hezzy, and Mike are well-liked back in Reliable. They got fine brides in Eunice, Lois, and Tempy, too. Done quite well out there."

"Knew they would." Abner gave a decisive nod. "Micah writes 'bout how holpful you Chance boys have bin." He slapped them each on the shoulder and pulled them close for a moment. "Yore like family to them. I cain't tell you how beholden I am to you an' yourn."

As quick as the emotion came on, it was over. Abner clapped his hat back on and took them inside for some dinner.

Logan and Bryce grinned. They'd made the right choice in coming.

thirteen

"Y'all come back now, ya hear?" Abner MacPherson waved them off after an early breakfast the next morning.

"Yes, sir," Logan and Bryce answered dutifully as they rode out of the yard and turned onto the road. They'd decided to make an early start so they could stop by the Hawk's Fall General Store. Hattie had asked them to check to see if they had any messages. Logan hoped they did—he wanted to know about the mysterious "matter" they'd written to Lovejoy about.

"Abner's a good man," Bryce mused.

"True." Logan couldn't argue with that. "I'm glad we came, but it's nice to be getting back."

"Funny how quick Miz Willow's place feels kinda like home." Bryce gave him a slanted look. "I reckon Hattie has a lot to do with it."

"They both do." Logan wasn't sure what Bryce was getting at, but something warned him not to probe. Hattie was an upstanding woman, considerate hostess, devoted healer, kind spirit, and good friend. She couldn't help being pretty, so he wouldn't let that dampen his appreciation of her fine qualities one bit. He shot Bryce a smile. "Speaking of Miz Willow and Hattie, I have an idea."

❧

"Cut it out!" Bryce cracked one eye open to glower at him.

"Sure." Logan watched his brother close his eye again and try to burrow under the covers. He flicked more water. "Soon as you get up!"

"You can't blame a guy for wanting to prolong the best night's sleep he's had in three days." Bryce flung back his blankets. "After all, I had to sleep with your feet in my face in that loft!"

"And your feet were in mine. It was the only way we could both lie down without one of us running the risk of rollin' off." Logan started to shave. "We've got church this morning, so we'll meet the rest of the people from the holler. You'd best get going."

"All right, all right." Bryce rummaged through the trunk to pull out their Sunday best.

"What're you doin'?" Logan stopped him. "We've got to muck out the barn before we get dressed for church. Come on."

While they worked, Hattie came out to gather eggs. Logan stopped for a minute to look at her. Something was different. . . .

"What'd you do to your hair?" He blurted the question before he had a chance to stop himself. It was none of his business how she wore her hair. But it was all scraped back and pinned up so tight. Where was her long dancing braid the color of a sunrise?

"Hmmm?" Hattie shut the chicken coop and raised a hand to smooth back her hair. "Is it coming down?"

"No," Logan muttered. "It just looks different, is all."

"Of course it does!" She smiled at him and Bryce. "I cain't go to the Lord's house with my hair hangin' down my back in a braid. That's only passable for a young gal." She went to get the pail of milk since Logan had made a habit of doing that chore for her.

"You are young." Bryce joined the conversation.

"Kind of you to say so, but I'm no spring chicken." Hattie picked up the pail. "I'm a widow."

How did I manage to forget that she's had a husband? Maybe because she's like no widow I've ever met. I reckon scrapin' back your crowning glory isn't so awful when you're of Miz Willow's age, but Hattie? Now that's a crime.

"You both come on inside when yore finished here. Breakfast'll be on the table." With that, she left.

Telling himself it was a good thing she was gone so he couldn't stick his foot in his mouth again, Logan focused on the work at hand. He finished mucking out the stalls, then climbed the ladder to change. By the time he and Bryce left the barn, his stomach was growling.

As he filled up on country-fried potatoes and poached eggs, Logan reconsidered Hattie's Sunday getup. Her green dress wasn't faded like the yellow and blue he'd seen her wear for everyday, and it swirled a little at the bottom edge when she turned around. He still didn't like her hair pinned up, but the style did show off her slender neck and little ears. He was just wondering whether or not she could still carry her knife when she caught him looking.

"Ahem." He cleared his throat and turned to Miz Willow. "Couldn't help but notice how nice you ladies look this morning." He smiled at both of them.

"Thankee, Logan." Miz Willow beamed and smoothed the white wisps escaping her bun. "Nice of you to notice. I reckon everyone'll be gussied up today. Hattie and me need to hold our own."

Hattie shook her head but patted the old woman's hand. "You'd shore give any fella a run for his money iff'n he came sniffin' around, Miz Willow. But I wouldn't know what to do without you, so don't be gettin' any crazy notions."

"Heh, heh." The widow slapped her knee. "That I would, dearie. That I would." She smiled fondly at Hattie. "But I won't be batting my eyelashes at any whippersnapper who smiles my way."

Logan couldn't help but think Miz Willow wasn't the widow he'd like to hear that promise from.

❧

It was a fairly short walk to the schoolhouse where they held church every Sunday. Hattie walked beside Miz Willow, holding her arm to keep her steady on the uneven road. Logan and Bryce walked on each side of them.

They were looking mighty handsome this morning. Hattie wasn't quite sure whether she'd forgotten how good-looking the brothers were while they were at Hawk's Fall or if it was their Sunday clothes.

When they got to the schoolhouse, women would be swarming all around them. Logan and Bryce's visit would be the high point of the year—whether or not they ended up hitched.

She knew they wouldn't. She loved the holler and wouldn't dream of leaving it, but Logan and Bryce were used to finer manners. She was well aware of how unpolished they all sounded, but these were her people. She knew Logan and Bryce were glad to visit, but the holler would never be home to them the way Chance Ranch was.

A crowd of people milled around the front of the building, and Hattie could tell when everybody caught sight of the Chance brothers. They stopped talking for a minute, then started whispering furiously.

Silk Trevor came up to them immediately, her husband and sons close on her heels. After a warm welcome—hugs for Hattie and Miz Willow from Silk and a lot of shoulder slapping and hand shaking among the men. Mary Pleasant came up to join them. Her husband, Asa, would be filling in for the circuit-riding parson today.

Hattie saw Nessie walking from the distance and motioned for her to come over. Rooster was nowhere in sight, as he hadn't been for the past two Sundays. Hattie hoped he would show up today after his first meeting with Logan and Bryce.

Lizzie and Sky Pleasant stood over with the Cleary sisters and a few other young ladies. At least they knew to wait for an introduction. After the service, everyone would stay around to chat and laugh before heading home to supper. Then she could introduce the Chances to Otis Nye and Li'l Nate Rucker—not to mention the Clearys.

They all moved into the schoolhouse, where benches formed rows down the narrow room. Hattie steered Nessie to her and Miz Willow's customary bench. Since Nessie's sister Goody had married up and joined the Peasley pew, Lovejoy had gone to California, and Rooster had stopped attending regularly, there wasn't a Linden bench any longer.

With the Chance men, it was a much tighter fit than usual, but they managed. Asa stood at the front and opened with prayer before asking them to rise.

His deep baritone led them in "Forth in Thy Name." The hymn, one of Hattie's favorites, swelled in the small schoolhouse:

"The task Thy wisdom hath assigned,
O let me cheerfully fulfill;
In all my works Thy presence find,
And prove Thy good and perfect will."

She loved the way a hymn could speak for so many. Every person had a task, but each was different. The words encouraged her, calling her to be a healer. When Hattie helped ease suffering or bring new life into the holler, she knew she was serving to carry out God's will.

Asa led them in "My Hope Is Built." The men and women sang in turns and joining in the chorus:

"On Christ the solid Rock I stand,
All other ground is sinking sand. . . ."

Hattie could hear Logan's rumble from where he sat on Miz Willow's left. The way his deep voice melded with her higher notes reminded Hattie that harmony came in many different forms.

The Chance brothers sounded different from the folks of the holler, but in the Lord, they all were joined in the family of God.

fourteen

Logan could pick out Hattie's soft soprano alongside Miz Willow's wavery alto. As they all worshipped, he was struck by the power of God's love to join people together in the bonds of faith. These folks weren't only part of Logan's adventure—they were part of God's plan for his life. He just didn't know how. The uncertainty made him shift a little on the bench as Asa began the sermon on the Sixteenth Psalm. He was glad Asa had chosen to speak on one of King David's psalms—the verses of praise in the Word of God never failed to give him focus. Asa talked for a bit on the joy and hope of having the Lord's guidance before reading directly from the Scriptures.

"Verse eleven is David praising God directly: 'Thou wilt shew me the path of life: in thy presence is fulness of joy; at thy right hand there are pleasures for evermore.'" Asa paused for a moment to let those words sink in before expounding on them. "We cain only fulfill our purpose iff'n we follow the path God lays for us. Only then can we feel the full joy of His presence in our lives and be firm in our hope for the future."

And there it was. Logan sat up a bit straighter. He'd follow the path as far as he could see and trust the Lord for whatever lay beyond the next curve. Not knowing what came next was a part of the adventure, but knowing God controlled it was part of life.

Asa closed in prayer, and the service ended. Everyone stood up and shuffled toward the door. People milled around, catching up with the families they didn't see during the course of the week. Tiny girls with string bows in their pigtails took turns on the swings and seesaw while young boys chased each other, stopping only to pick up their hats when they fell off.

Hattie braced Miz Willow's arm and walked over to Abigail Rucker, gesturing for them to follow her. A hulking man stood protectively next to the heavily expectant woman. Logan wondered if he was her brother, since he remembered Hattie saying Abigail's husband was little.

"Logan and Bryce Chance, you've already met Abigail Rucker." Hattie nodded toward the giant. "This is her husband, Li'l Nate."

Little? There was nothing tiny about the man whose beefy hand all but squeezed the life out of Logan's in a hearty shake.

"Nice to meet you both." Li'l Nate beamed. "Abby told me you'd come to town. Wish I'd been around when you stopped by, but I was working at the smithy."

"You're the blacksmith." That made sense.

"Why do they call you Li'l Nate?" Bryce's curiosity got the better of him.

"Big Nate were my pa and the blacksmith afore me." Li'l Nate grinned. "It's from when I were growin' up, and it jist stuck."

"Li'l Nate's the best harmonica player in these hills." Hattie turned to him. "Logan and Bryce got two shiny new harmonicas but don't know how to work 'em."

"I'd be tickled to teach you boys," Not-So-Li'l Nate offered.

"Thanks!" Logan and Bryce answered in unison.

"Why don't you and Abigail come on back to our place for Sunday supper?" Miz Willow invited. "It'd break up yore walk a bit, an' you could give 'em a few pointers. Otis Nye'll be joinin' us."

"Thankee kindly." Abigail rested her hands on her back. "I'd be glad to eat someone else's cookin'!"

While that was settled, Logan saw a thick-waisted woman with salt-and-pepper hair make a beeline toward them. She all but shoved Hattie to one side to break into the circle.

"Mornin', Miz Willow." The woman gazed at him and Bryce out of the corner of her eye. "I see yore visitors came back from Hawk's Fall," she simpered.

"Yore right at that, Bethilda." Miz Willow's eyes twinkled. "Bethilda Cleary, meet Logan and Bryce Chance from Californy."

"Nice to meet you." Logan and Bryce took off their hats. Logan watched in disbelief as the woman sank into an awkward curtsy.

"Pleased to make yore acquaintance, sirs." Bethilda gave an unctuous grin. "It's shore a pleasure to have fine gentlemen visit our humble holler. Shame we didn't meet sooner." She shot a quick glare at Hattie.

Logan could see Bryce shift next to Li'l Nate, whose eyebrows reached near his hairline. One thing was clear: Bethilda Cleary was not the most pleasant of the holler inhabitants. But what could she want from them?

"I had hoped you handsome brothers would take an invite to Sunday supper so my family could get to know you."

Logan followed her gaze to a pair of young girls. One couldn't have been more than fourteen.

Bryce wouldn't look at Bethilda, and Logan saw Hattie shaking her head slightly but urgently. Now he saw which way the wind blew, and it was time to get out of the draft.

"Thank you for thinking of us, but we've already made arrangements." Logan kept the refusal as polite as possible.

"Oh, well, Miz Willow and Hattie won't mind, I'm shore." Bethilda trilled a fake laugh and shot another glare toward Hattie. "They've had you all to theyselves, haven't they?"

"No, ma'am. We've been meeting up with kin and have gotten to know the Trevors, Pleasants, and MacPhersons," Logan ground out. It was obvious the woman wanted to accuse Hattie of setting her cap for one of them. Ridiculous. Hattie was the one who had warned them about the likes of Bethilda Cleary.

"Spent half our time in Hawk's Fall," Logan went on. "And even if our plans only concerned Miz Willow and Hattie—"

"Which they don't," Bryce tacked on.

"We'd be hard-pressed to give up their company," Logan finished.

"I see." A steely glint lit Bethilda's gaze.

"I'm to learn 'em on the harmonica, Miz Cleary." Li'l Nate steered her attention to himself. "So as they'll be ready for the doin's."

"Wonderful!" Bethilda was all smiles once again. "But we must see you before Friday a week. Why don't you boys stop on by fer—"

"I'm shore they'll be seein' you, Bethilda." Hattie interrupted what was sure to have been another invitation and steered Abigail Rucker to the path. "We'd best git on our way now."

Logan smiled his thanks. There wouldn't be any way for them to refuse a second time, and the last thing he and Bryce wanted was to be stuck with Bethilda Cleary and her daughters.

Hattie smiled as she mashed the taters, remembering the look on Bethilda's face when Logan and Bryce had refused her invitation. The woman had become so biggity she needed to be taken down a peg or two. Hattie knew Bethilda would make her sorry she'd interrupted, but she couldn't stand there and let the woman trap Logan and Bryce when Logan had stood up for her and Miz Willow like that—not that they couldn't take care of themselves, of course.

Abigail sat in the rocking chair, stroking her burgeoning belly and watching Otis Nye carve another perfect checker. The old man seemed gruff and crotchety most of the time, but underneath he just wanted to be useful. If only he'd stop carving those ugly owls of his and giving folks the stink eye when they couldn't think of anything nice to say about them.

Miz Willow put the biscuits in the ash oven and checked on the pot roast. She handed Hattie salt and butter to add to the potatoes. Hattie had already skimmed the cream from the top of the milk and poured it in. Soon enough, she was setting honey, butter, and jam on the table.

"Come on in now," Miz Willow hollered out the window at the men. "Dinner's ready."

Li'l Nate trailed Logan and Bryce to the washbasin. They'd been digging a hole for a pole they'd chosen for horseshoes. Bryce had remembered some old ones in the barn, and they'd decided to get up a game before the meal.

"Pass the taters," Otis grumbled at Li'l Nate, who was in the middle of taking another huge helping. It was a good thing Hattie had mashed about two dozen. She'd planned on making tater cakes with the leftovers but could see that wouldn't be happening.

"Shore are good vittles, ain't they?" Li'l Nate passed them on.

Otis sopped up some taters and gravy with a biscuit before grunting, "Passable."

Coming from Otis Nye, that was high praise.

"I say it's mighty fine eatin'." Bryce shoved some pork roast into his mouth and chewed emphatically.

"Right you are." Abigail took a sip of her milk and patted

her tummy. "Babe's kickin' to make room for more." She grabbed Otis's hand and laid it on her stomach. He tried to pull away, but surprise flashed in his rheumy eyes as he felt the babe kick, and the lines around his mouth softened.

"Gonna be a strong 'un, Nate." Otis spoke the first compliment Hattie had ever heard from him. "You gonna make a fine mama, Abigail." Then he pokered up again. "Those biscuits ain't gonna et themselves, boy." He poked Logan in the ribs. "Give 'em over."

Hattie saw Logan bite back a grin as he followed the grumpy old-timer's command. Otis Nye's crotchety outside hid a soft spot wider than he'd like to admit. He was the exact opposite of Bethilda Cleary, whose fake smiles hid dark thoughts. Hattie would rather see Otis Nye any day of the week.

Dinner ended, but nobody was ready to leave the table.

"Yore food done broke m' breadbasket." Otis Nye glowered at them while he snatched the last biscuit and slathered it with honey.

"Yep. Between yore vittles and his child"—Abigail patted Nate's shoulder—"I'm thinkin' I'm too big to git up agin."

"Yore eatin' for two, Abby." Nate beamed at his tiny wife. "But I ken what you mean. I'm too stuffed to play a harmonica. Gonna have to let the food settle a mite."

"I'm with you on that," Logan agreed, and Bryce nodded.

Hattie got up to brew some coffee and then sat back down. She loved Sundays, the day the Lord Himself had set aside to enjoy hearty meals and good company.

fifteen

Logan and Bryce waved good-bye to Hattie and Miz Willow after breakfast a few days later. The Trevor boys were going to take them hunting, and they would meet halfway at the schoolhouse.

We've been here a week already, and this is the first time we're going out into the countryside together, just the men. We'll tromp around the hills all day, track animals, and maybe bring home supper. This is more like it!

"Nice day for huntin'," Ted said in greeting when they arrived. Or was it Fred? Logan couldn't really tell. Both of the twins wore brown buckskin trousers and cambric shirts faded gray from many washings.

"Sure is, Fred," Bryce agreed. Logan shot him a quick look. Was he bluffing, or did he really know which brother was which?

"We figgured we'd go up aways, then double back on the meadow an' see if we cain't stay upwind of some deer." The other one—Logan decided it had to be Ted since they hadn't corrected Bryce—rocked back on his heels. Logan looked him over and tried to find a way to distinguish between the two. Impossible.

Bryce and Logan followed them up the trail for a while before cutting off into the forest. Logan gave up trying to tell them apart. It seemed as though he'd be doing a fair bit of mumbling—at least their names both ended with *ed.*

The two of them kept up a running dialogue as they passed various landmarks, keeping Logan smiling at the stories they told.

"That's where Uncle Asa got chased by Otis Nye's old ram. Ended up sprawled on the ground a few times afore he clambered up that thar tree." They pointed out a Fraser fir to their right. "Shore were a sight—that goat were as cantankerous as his owner."

A little farther in, they showed off a small cave in the mountainside. "Here's where we tracked the red fox as was killin' off our layin' hens."

After a while, they left off talking. Logan realized they must be getting close to the place where the twins had last seen the deer. Sure enough, they could catch glimpses of the meadow just a little ways off. The twins led them to a huge fallen log where they hunkered down to wait.

It was long past noon before anything moved. A few rabbits hopped around the clover, but they held off. One shot and no other animal would come near the meadow again. Then they saw it. A young buck, judging by his antlers, crossed the meadow kitty-corner to them. It put its nose out to test the air, but they were downwind.

Ever so slowly, they all aimed, careful not to move quickly and scare it off. They shared silent nods and fired within seconds of each other. The buck fell immediately, and they hurried over. If they hadn't shot it in the head or heart, they needed to put it out of its pain as quickly as they could.

It was a clean kill, though, so they set to work. They picked out a fallen branch big enough to do the job and lashed the deer to it. They took turns, two at a time, holding either end of the branch to carry it back down the mountain. It was just the beginning of summer, so the buck hadn't had a chance to fatten up like it would have managed by fall. All the same, it was big enough to fill their need.

After they dressed it, the Trevor boys would take half home and leave half for Miz Willow, Hattie, Logan, and

Bryce. It was a good start toward restocking the healers' larder, Logan realized. He and his brother had sadly depleted the smokehouse.

The women would stretch and cure the hide to make deerskin pouches for their herbs or scrape it thin to cover windows. The sinews would be dried and used as twine. Nothing would go to waste.

❧

Stooping to harvest useful plants, Hattie sang a verse of "Fairest Lord Jesus":

"Fair are the meadows, fairer still the woodlands,
Robed in the blooming garb of spring;
Jesus is fairer, Jesus is purer,
Who makes the woeful heart to sing."

The world around her was teeming with life and the things to sustain it. Today Hattie was looking for particular yarbs. The warm months always brought on rashes and poison ivy, so she'd need jewelweed and marshmallow for sure. She'd already added to her supply of yarbs to help with childbearing, and they were well set for coughs and fevers. It was a healer's duty to be prepared for everything possible.

After breakfast when Logan and Bryce had left to meet up with the Trevor twins, Miz Willow had given her a list of things to look for. From the plants listed and what Hattie knew of their uses, she had an idea why she was gathering them.

Dandelion root cleaned out the body and purified. Elderberry leaf was good for headaches. Milk thistle was a help for poisoning, whether snake, spider, plant, or drink. Lady slipper root took care of pain and sleep. Peppermint soothed the stomach, and scouring rush cleaned the bladder. Evening primrose could help with moodiness and ease the need for liquor in some.

The last one tipped the scale. Miz Willow was preparing for Rooster Linden. He hadn't come by yet as he'd promised, but they reckoned it was only a matter of time. Sooner or later, he'd make himself so sick, his body and his soul would overrule his habit—and when that happened, they'd be ready with all the help they could offer.

Gathering all of the necessary plants took Hattie through most of the holler, but she didn't mind. These were her very favorite kinds of days. Fluffy clouds moseyed along in the bright blue sky like they had all the time in the world to pass the mountains guarding the horizon. Everything around her was green and thriving. Birds sang to the bees in the blossoms. Flitterbirds sipped from the flowers just long enough to be seen, and butterflies danced along a breeze to tickle the tall grasses.

The sun warmed Hattie's hair and neck when she wasn't under the cool trees. When she took out her sack lunch of cheese and bread, she chose to sit near the stream. The water burbled along, clear and inviting. Hattie took off her shoes and dangled her toes in the cold water, flinging drops into the air to catch the light before they rippled back into the brook.

God was everywhere around her, just shining His love through beautiful things. This was her home, her holler. She could only wonder if Logan and Bryce Chance saw how special and precious it truly was.

"I'm glad yore back, Hattie-mine." Miz Willow pulled the door shut and waved a letter at her. "Lovejoy done writ us back, and I've been waitin' on you." The old woman practically danced around the cabin.

"All right. Let's hear—wait a minute." Hattie peered out the window. "Where're the menfolk?"

"They shot a buck up the mountain with the Trevor boys and brought it back here to butcher it. They took the horses and carried half of it all back to the Trevor place. They left awhile ago, so they'll be comin' home soon. I've already got venison stew ready and simmerin' in the pot, and corn bread keepin' warm in the fire." She pushed the letter into Hattie's hands. "Go on an' read it. I cain't keep still after that much waitin'!"

Hattie opened the envelope and began to read aloud:

Dear Hattie and Miz Willomena,

I shore was shocked when I got yore last letter. I don't know 'bout any trunk in the barn nor any carved wooden box. It's a mark of what fine folk live in the ole holler that you done tole me instead of puttin' what you found to use.

By now you've spent enough time with Logan and Bryce to see what manner of family I've taken on and to know you cain trust 'em as much as I do. So I'm gonna ask you on yore honor to give it all to them. The Lord will show them what to do with it. It's a jump of faith, but I know you both been stretchin' yore legs all yore life!

Yore in my heart,
Lovejoy

"That's shore a relief." Hattie refolded the letter and handed it back to Miz Willow.

"It's a good decision, I reckon." Miz Willow nodded. "So when we gonna tell 'em?"

"After supper, I'd say." Hattie went over to the fire.

Someone knocked on the door.

"Did someone say 'supper'?" Logan's voice sounded so hopeful, Hattie had to smile.

"Yep. Come on in." Miz Willow put the letter in her pocket, and Logan and Bryce tromped in.

"Good. I'm so hungry, I could eat Bryce's cooking." Logan grinned at the outraged look on Bryce's face.

"Hey! You've got no call to—" Bryce thought for a moment before giving a sheepish grin. "Nah, there's some truth in it."

"Set down, then." Miz Willow shook her head at their antics. They were just like the Peasley young'uns, scrapping around for a laugh.

Once the prayer was said, the food eaten, and the dishes cleared away, Logan went to bring out the checkerboard Otis Nye had made for them.

"Beautiful piece." Bryce ran his hands around the smooth pine board checkered with walnut stain and varnished over to gleam in the light.

"These, too." Logan held up one of the stained checkers and fingered the carved crown on the top. "Good craftsmanship. You've gotta give him credit—Otis Nye knows his way around a whittlin' knife."

"Shore does. It'd do him good to hear you say it." Miz Willow rocked. "But now's not the time for checkers. Why don't you both sit down for a minute, and we'll have us a little chat."

Logan shot Hattie a quizzical glance, but she refused to give him an inkling of what was to come. The widow would have it out in her own good time.

"Now when we heard you boys was a-comin' to Salt Lick Holler, Hattie here went and cleared up the barn an' loft for yore sleepin' space. Do you follow?"

"And a nice job she did, too," Logan praised.

"Real comfortable." Bryce nodded.

"What you might not know is that this ain't my property. Lovejoy didn't move in with me—I came to her home when it looked like she'd be marryin' up with yore brother. So when Hattie found a trunk in the loft—you know what trunk I mean?"

"Yes."

As Logan and Bryce agreed, Hattie could see interest light their eyes. They'd figured the general way things were headed.

"She came across a few things. I'll let her take it from here." Miz Willow leaned back and clasped her hands together as Logan and Bryce turned to stare at Hattie.

"I found a leather sack and a wooden box," Hattie elaborated. "We opened 'em both, and the sack held some leather scraps. But the box was somethin' we had to write Lovejoy 'bout."

"It's what we hoped Lovejoy would've written about in her letter to us that you boys brung on yore trip," the widow broke in. "But it hadn't been enough time."

"Today we finally got word from her about it." Hattie handed Logan the letter and watched as he and Bryce read it silently.

"So we're supposed to see to whatever's in the box," Logan prompted.

"Right you are. So we're honorin' her wishes." Hattie put the box on the table and opened the lid.

sixteen

Logan stared at the open box in front of him without speaking.

"Go on and shut that thing, Logan," Bryce ordered. "You've been lookin' at it since we got up here." He tapped on the loft wall. "It hasn't changed any, so stop lookin' at it, and let's talk about what we're gonna do with it."

Logan shut the lid on the money. Seventy-four dollars. It was a small fortune, and Lovejoy had just given it to them. But one thing bothered him. "Why didn't she tell Hattie and Miz Willow to keep it?"

"I dunno." Bryce shrugged. "But knowin' Lovejoy, she prayed on it before she made the decision. Like she wrote, the Lord will show us what to do with it."

"I don't think Lovejoy reckons we'll just keep it." The glimmerings of an idea sparked in Logan's imagination. "I think I might have a few things in mind."

"Good." Bryce put the box back in the trunk Hattie had found it in. "The way I see it, this is your adventure, Logan. I'm only along for the ride. I'm happy to help and curious about what you want to do, but that's the most I'm going to say on this subject."

"Lovejoy left it to both of us."

"And I'll help you with your plan, but I've got the feeling you're supposed to make the actual decision." Bryce pulled off his boots. "That's all there is to it."

"Fine." Logan shook his head in disbelief.

God must have a purpose for this money. And I'm supposed to find it.

"Bryce?" Logan wanted to run a few things by his brother. "I think we should use this money to help folks around here."

"Sounds like a good idea." Bryce paused. "Feels right. But how?"

"I don't think we should give it away to one person. I don't even believe we should divide the money evenly." Logan talked through his thoughts. "We should take a good long look at the people around here and what they really need."

"Makes sense." Bryce seemed excited by the idea. "But I don't think it's the type of thing where we just buy everyone some canned beans. We need to do something to help that will keep on helping after we're gone. Like the water pump you had us order for Hattie on our way home from Hawk's Fall."

"Yeah. Yeah, that's good." Logan chewed the inside of his lip and concentrated. "That's improving on something they already have, though."

"So what do the people of Salt Lick Holler have that can be used to make their lives better?"

❧

Friday afternoon arrived far too quickly to Hattie's way of thinking. Where was the summer going? It seemed as though spring had barely begun, but here they were in June. She changed into her Sunday best to get ready for the doings. She figured it ought to be a lot of fun.

She helped Miz Willow put her hair up into a pretty snow-white twist and gave her another cup of burdock root tea. She'd be sitting on those hard benches for a while, and Hattie didn't want her rheumatism acting up. For good measure, she'd bring some more to the sang. Otis Nye might have use of some later on, and it wouldn't be noticed with everybody bringing something to share.

When the menfolk knocked on the door, Hattie handed Miz Willow her shawl and cloak. "It'll be evenin' afore we come back." She handed Bryce and Logan a pan of apple cobbler each before picking up her own cloak and satchel. With everybody excited by the doings, there would like as not be a few bumps and bruises. She'd be ready.

"Mmmm." Bryce sniffed the cobbler. "I say we stay right here and eat these ourselves."

"And you the guests of honor." Miz Willow waggled her finger. "Now don't you be tryin' to sneak a taste, neither."

"We would never!" Somehow Logan managed to sound affronted even as he chewed a piece of the crumb topping he'd broken off.

"Rascal." Miz Willow shook her head.

Hattie thought Miz Willow had the right of it. Logan Chance might be handsome, mannerly, and charming, but there was still a bit of the scamp about him. A woman had to be careful about that. She thought of Nessie's husband, a good-natured scapegrace who'd ducked out on her a year after the wedding. It just went to show—a boy made a mess; a man made a marriage.

Not that her opinion mattered much. As they drew near the schoolhouse, Hattie could see that every young gal from here to Hawk's Fall was already in attendance. It would be an interesting afternoon.

Hattie steered Miz Willow over to a bench along the side of the schoolhouse so she'd be able to lean back. She tucked her satchel under the bench and took the cobblers from Logan and Bryce.

"You two go on and chat around before the sangin' starts," Hattie said, leaving them to go put the cobblers on one of the tables set up for vittles. The tables were heaped full of bread, biscuits, corn pone, deviled eggs, mashed potatoes, green beans, carrots, stews, a couple of baked chickens, and one suckling pig. Jars of jams and honey sat alongside crocks of butter and pitchers of fresh milk. Pies, muffins, and cake sat off to one side where Hattie put the cobblers, too. It looked as though everyone had gone all-out for the occasion.

The younger boys were putting together a bonfire in the middle of the wide circle of benches. They'd light it after the eating was done and before the singing began. By then it would be getting nippy, and the sun wouldn't stay out too long. She cast a look around to see if anyone was missing.

Miz Willow was chatting with Silk Trevor. Abigail and Katherine were comparing notes, trying to decide which babe would come first. Hattie would reckon on Kat for that—her first two had been quick births. The twins were playing the spoons—on each other's heads to make the children laugh. She didn't see Logan and Bryce right away—they were surrounded by a whole passel of folk.

What did she expect? After all, the Chance brothers were the main attraction here today. Just because she wouldn't set her cap for them didn't mean others didn't plan to. She could only hope Logan and Bryce didn't return their regard.

❧

"These are m' daughters," Bethilda Cleary said, clutching Logan's arm like a dog with a bone. Bryce had wisely slid out of range, but loyalty kept him close.

Lily and Lark made awkward imitations of the curtsy their mother had made the previous Sunday. He and Bryce tipped their hats, but the girls looked disappointed. Had they honestly expected bows?

"Nice to meet you, Mr. Chance. Mr. Chance." The younger one, Lark, giggled.

"We heard tell this is yore very first sang," Lily chimed in. "We'll be happy to git you anything you need."

"We brung the possum stew o'er yonder." Lark sidled closer. "I'd be happy to fetch you some."

"Maybe later." Logan pasted a smile on his face and looked around for a reason—any reason—to leave.

"My gals cook up a fine mess o' vittles." Bethilda smiled so widely Logan could count her teeth.

Lily was trying to talk to Bryce, who took a step back for every step she came closer. Any farther and he'd be cornered against the schoolhouse. Logan would've stepped in, but he was surrounded by Bethilda and Lark. He looked around out of pure desperation and caught the eye of one of the twins. Fred or Ted—Logan didn't care which—sauntered on over and managed to step between Lily and Bethilda to snag his arm. Logan saw the other Trevor walking over to Bryce.

"Ted and I need to talk to you Chance boys for a minute. I'm shore the Clearys will excuse you." Fred pulled Logan away before the women had a chance to protest.

When they were safely on the other side of the circle, Fred clapped him on the back. Ted burst out laughing. "Didn't anybody see fit to warn you 'bout that Bethilda Cleary?"

"Yeah. Pa'll sic his dogs on you iff'n you upset him, but Bethilda'll set her daughters after you!"

"I'm gonna ignore that since you helped us out of a tight spot." Logan grinned.

"Yeah." Bryce still looked a bit harried.

"No problem. 'Sides, Uncle Asa's 'bout to say grace so we cain tuck in."

By now Logan had lost track of which twin was speaking.

"Iff'n you know which thing the Clearys brung, keep away from it," one advised.

"Stew," Bryce said, casting a dubious glance at the kettle.

Asa called everyone to attention to say grace, and then people began to crowd around the food. Logan noticed that the women and children hung back, waiting for the men to finish. When he got to the table, he saw that most of the corn bread was gone, so he put two pieces on his plate alongside chicken, mashed potatoes, and green beans. He planned to have a healthy helping of Hattie's apple cobbler later on.

He and Bryce went over to where Miz Willow and Hattie were sitting and gestured for the Trevor family and the Ruckers to come join them. There were no seats available on either side of them when Bethilda led her daughters over. No one responded when she glowered around at the people taking up the three benches, much less offered to make room. Logan let out a deep breath when they huffed away.

As they were eating, Logan tipped a piece of corn bread onto Miz Willow's plate, then passed one to Hattie. He knew it was her favorite, and he'd been right to think it would be gone before she got there. She flashed him a surprised look, then a grateful smile.

"Thankee."

"Anytime." He smiled and leaned back. *This might just turn out to be a fun evening.*

After their early supper, the men gathered around to toss horseshoes and play checkers in the waning light while the women cleared up the tables—not that they had to take care of anything except dirty dishes. Not a speck of food was left in sight.

"Yeah!" Logan whooped as his horseshoe ringed the pole.

"Come on, everybody back to yore seats," Asa called out, ringing a bell to make everybody listen. "We're 'bout ready to light the bonfire."

Everyone quickly went back to the seats they'd taken for supper, but Logan didn't see Hattie. Lily and Lark looked at him and Bryce, and the men immediately sprawled out a little, taking up the whole bench. One of the boys lit the bonfire, and in the light it cast, Logan could see Hattie. She crouched in front of a little girl, spreading something on her hand and drying her tears. While the musicians tuned their instruments, she gave the child a hug and sent her scampering back to her mother. *She has such a big heart, my Hattie.*

My Hattie? When did she become mine?

seventeen

Logan pushed the disquieting thought aside as Hattie walked toward them and nudged Bryce to scoot over so she could sit between him and Miz Willow. She smiled and wiggled in, adjusting the cloak behind the older widow's back to make her more comfortable.

"What was wrong with the kid?" Logan nodded toward the little girl, now snuggled on her mama's lap.

"She took a tumble and scratched her hand." Hattie tucked her medicine satchel back beneath the bench. "I cleaned it and put some marshmallow salve on to take away some of the sting."

They stopped talking as the musicians began to play. Most were like no musicians Logan had ever seen. They sat scattered around the bonfire, so noise came from all sides. Fred and Ted rattled the washboard and boinged a mouth harp with youthful vigor. Rooster, who'd shown up just in time for the food, blew into a good-sized jug to add hollow hoots to the tune of Asa's fiddle. Otis Nye clacked on a pair of spoons with surprising energy and skill, while Silk plucked the strings of a simple dulcimer. Next to Logan, Li'l Nate wailed on his harmonica, making sweet music on the instrument so tiny in his big hands.

All together, they made the music lively and loud. Logan didn't know too many of the songs, but he pitched in when he could. Most of time he clapped along with the music, stomping his feet when his hands stung from the evening air and too much clapping.

"Any requests?" Rooster took a nip from the flask in his pocket and swayed a little on his tree stump.

"Equinoxial and Phoebe!" A woman called out. Logan didn't recognize her voice or the name of the song, so he sat back to listen:

"Equinoxial swore by the green leaves on the tree
He could do more work in a day
Than Phoebe could do in three.

"So little Phoebe said to him, 'This you must allow.
You can do the work in the house and
I'll go follow the plow. . . .' "

Logan couldn't help laughing as the song progressed. The man got kicked in the head by the brindle cow, slipped in the pigs' mud, set the food on fire, and lost the hen before his wife came home. The last verse summed it all up:

"Now Equinoxial says, looking up to heaven,
Phoebe could do more work in a day
Than he could do in seven!"

A great burst of laughter erupted from the circle, the women nodding vigorously as the men shook their heads and rolled their eyes. For his part, Logan saw the truth behind the words—not that women could do more than men, although some could, but that men didn't always value how hard women worked to hold everything together.

Hattie, for example, cooked, cleaned, laundered, sewed, and tended to the livestock like any housewife. In addition, she gathered, dried, crushed, and combined all the plants and things she used to heal the people around here. Hattie did with care and skill what he hoped to do with money—use the things the people in the holler already had to better their lives. If he did half as much good as Hattie managed, he'd have used the money well.

The musicians took a break, and people got up to stretch their legs. Logan went to get a drink of water and saw Hattie off to his right, cuddling a bundled baby. The smile on her face glowed brighter than the bonfire itself.

"Such a shame," Bethilda Cleary sidled up to his left.

Serves you right for not keeping on guard, Logan chided himself ruefully.

"What's a shame?" he asked as he wondered how he could get away before her daughters joined them.

"Hattie, of course." Bethilda widened her eyes. "Oh, I thought you knew." She made a *tsk-tsk* noise. "The way she's been hogging you, and now you cain't take yore eyes off her. . . ." The woman's voice trailed off as she shook her head.

"Hattie Thales is a good woman." Logan bristled. "She's been kind enough to introduce me and Bryce to everyone around."

"So yore not castin' glances at her?" Bethilda's eyes narrowed in challenge.

"I was just noticing how no matter where I go, women will always gather around a baby." Logan shrugged.

"True," Bethilda said, smirking. "Especially ones who cain't have their own."

Logan stalked away from the malicious woman and sank back down onto the bench, crossing his arms and scowling as Lily and Lark looked to come near.

So that's why Hattie hasn't married again. She can't have children. What's wrong with the men in these parts? Don't they have eyes to see that Hattie's a prize in and of herself?

Otis growled at them to name a song, and a few hesitant suggestions cropped up.

"'The Old Maid's Song,'" Bethilda ordered, gazing directly at Hattie.

Logan leaned close to Hattie to try to make out the words of the song. Was it his imagination, or did he see a flash of sadness in those beautiful blue eyes?

The song moved through several verses about the type of man a maid wouldn't marry. Only unmarried women sang these, with the rest of the town repeating the refrain. He watched Hattie without her noticing as she sang the last verse with a wistful smile.

"But I will marry a man that's kind,
Who's honest and wise
And will always be mine. . . ."

Then the refrain answered back:

"Then you'll not marry at all, at all,
Then you'll not marry at all."

Logan frowned at the words, which seemed to imply that no such man existed, or that if he did, he wouldn't want to marry the maid.

Says who?

As they walked home, Hattie stayed quiet. Too much was turning over in her mind—like the way the Cleary sisters made eyes at Logan and Bryce all evening. But she'd been expecting that. What she hadn't expected was for Logan to be so attentive. It was thoughtful of him to bring Miz Willow and her some corn bread—it was her favorite. And how had he come to know her so well, anyway?

She remembered the way the firelight lit his golden tan,

playing on his strong fingers as he clapped his hands to the music he didn't know. She wouldn't even have that memory but for the fact he'd saved her seat. She saw the way he'd elbowed Bryce to move over and make room.

He'd played the harmonica with more energy than accuracy that night and had a heap of fun trying out the washboard and spoons. The boy inside the thoughtful man came out and surprised her at times. Then he would look at her with a strange intensity, like when they sang "The Old Maid's Song." Why did it matter to her that he hadn't joined in the chorus?

You know very well why it matters, Hattie Thales. If he'd looked at you in the glow of the fire with his handsome blue eyes and ready smile and sang along, "Then you'll not marry at all, at all, then you'll not marry at all," whatever is left of the girl you once were would've just shriveled up and died.

The next two weeks rushed by more quickly as Hattie kept busy treating cuts, rashes, poison oak and ivy, turned ankles, and the run of typical summer maladies. Every time she was called away to some home or another, she was aware of an air of expectation before they realized Logan and Bryce weren't with her.

It wasn't only the single girls who liked having them around, either. The Trevor twins, who at the advanced age of nineteen still provided an impressive number of the scrapes she treated, were always coming by looking for the Chance brothers to go fishing, hunting, trapping, or swimming. Edward Trevor swore Bryce could help him tame the orneriest hound dog alive, and Li'l Nate always stood ready to whip out his harmonica and teach them a few bars. At every house she visited, the children tugged on her skirts, begging for Uncle Logan and Uncle Bryce to give them horsie rides or play hide and seek. Even ole Otis Nye growled at her to bring the boys by for a game of checkers when she dropped off the tea for his rheumatism.

It was enough to make a gal feel about as wanted as a tagalong younger sister who followed after the boys. Hattie wondered whether the Chance brothers knew how much they'd come to mean to Salt Lick Holler. She'd gladly tell them, but they were hardly ever home, and when they were, they kept her laughing too hard to remember. When they left, they'd take a piece of the holler with them and leave behind a gap in the lives of everyone they knew.

"We want to leave something behind that'll really change things around here." Logan paced in the loft—sort of. He managed about four steps one way before having to turn back around because of the slope of the roof.

"I thought we'd already gotten that far." Bryce stretched out on his pallet. "Hey, would ya quit walkin' over me?"

"Sure." Logan sat on the bench. "I'm edgy because we haven't gotten any further in deciding what to do with the money."

"Yep." Bryce nodded. "We've been kept pretty busy these past weeks."

"Don't I know it," Logan agreed. He'd hardly seen Hattie all week, with her out treating people and him and Bryce invited to so many houses.

"I like to think we're still doing some good," Bryce mused. "Those hound dogs of Ed's are shaping up to be a great bunch. He ought to fetch a fine price for them."

"True. I've never seen a dog obey so well as those pups." Logan raised his brows. "Ed vows it's all 'cuz of you, you know."

"I heard him say something like that." Bryce shrugged. "He's still the one who trains them. All I did was show him that rewarding the good behavior was a better track to take than punishing the bad. Dogs are like people—compliments over criticism."

"Only you could say something like that and make it sound right." Logan shook his head. "Well, you and maybe Otis Nye."

"Grumpy old geezer." Bryce smiled. "I think his carved owls are looking a lot better lately, since he doesn't make 'em tilted in the head anymore."

"And you've gotten a lot better at checkers." Logan winked at his brother. "Someday you might even beat me at it."

"Don't be so proud about how wily you are. It's not always a good thing to be so sly," Bryce warned. "But I don't mind losing. It's almost more fun to look at the game than to play it."

"Only because Otis is a craftsman with those checkers of his. Did you get a gander at the latest ones with the circles carved on the bottom?" Logan gave an appreciative whistle. "I don't know how he does it with that rheumatism of his."

"Hattie's tea helps a lot," Bryce thought aloud, "but I think it's mostly his legs that bother him. His knees crack and pop something awful."

"True. His hands are as quick as his tongue—just not as sharp!"

"Yeah." Bryce snorted. "Speaking of sharp, did you notice how often he has to put his whittling knife to the whetstone?"

"Now that you mention it"—Logan scratched his jaw—"I reckon that's because he puts it to such use."

"And has for some time." Bryce was quiet for a minute. "Do you think he whittles so much because he's alone a good portion of the time?"

"Could be." Logan frowned. "I wonder if he knows that Asa Pleasant has taken up whittling, too. They could sit together."

"That'd be a good idea. Asa's swan-necked towel pegs are sturdy and a little fancy," Bryce said, "but I'm most impressed by those nativities he hides in his shed."

"The detail on those figures is incredible," Logan added. "I was thinking of asking him to make a set to bring home for the mantel."

"That's a pretty tall order." Bryce shook his head.

"True." Logan remembered how detailed the sets had been. "And baby Jesus can actually come out of the manger and fit in Mary's arms! It must take him a long time to make all that—especially since he does it so perfectly."

"You can see the fur on the animals and expressions on the faces of the people," Bryce pointed out. "You should offer to pay him."

"Of course!" Logan couldn't believe Bryce thought he hadn't meant to pay Asa. "But I'm not sure how much would be appropriate. I don't want to suggest too little—it's his art—but if I offer too much money, he'll think I'm showing off or want to give him charity. Either way it'll sting his pride."

"That's the last thing you want. I guess you'll have to think about it." Bryce blew out the lantern, but Logan lay awake for a long while.

Lord, There's so much to think about. What do I offer Asa? How can I use the money to help the holler? They're such good people, but the last thing I want to do is offend them. They should be appreciated for the things they do and the way they live their lives upright in Your sight. So how do I encourage them and help at the same time?

eighteen

"Hattie! Hattie!"

Hattie reined Legs in at the sound of someone calling her name. She was just returning from a visit to the Peasleys, where Grandma had felt a hitch in her chest and had been struggling for air. Hattie had made hot tea of black cohosh root and coltsfoot leaf to open the lungs and help stop the coughing. After she rubbed on some of Miz Willow's eucalyptus and peppermint salve and had Grandma breathe in the vapors, the old lady was doing just fine.

"I'm so glad I caught you!" Mary Pleasant rushed up. "I done heard some terrible news. Daisy Thales's place burned down last night. Looks like Jamie knocked over a candle or sommat."

Hattie froze. Daisy was her sister-in-law—another Thales widow who lived in Hawk's Fall. Her son, Jamie, suffered from palsy. They already had so little, and now their house had burned down?

Why, Lord? Daisy tries so hard to be a good mama, staying up and tatting lace to make ends meet for her and her boy. I've wished they were closer, but this ain't the way I'd hoped for it to happen. Please be with them, Lord, in this difficult time.

"Was it just the house?" A cold fear seized Hattie's heart.

"Mostly. Daisy got Jamie out all right, but she went back to get her workbasket and Jamie's favorite blanket. She got out, but one of her arms is burnt. I don't know how bad. Nobody else was hurt, but a lot of folk pitched in to put out the fire and keep it from spreading."

"Thankee for tellin' me, Mary." Hattie couldn't quite manage a smile. "I've gotta go right now, you understand." She didn't even wait for Mary's assent as she urged Legs into a run.

The morning was half over already, and she needed to get home before she could set out to Hawk's Fall. It was usually almost a day's ride, but if she rode hard, she'd make it just before nightfall. When she got to the barn, Bryce was sitting outside, practicing his harmonica.

"Bryce!" Hattie slid off the horse. "There's been an emergency in Hawk's Fall, and I need to gather up some things and get there as fast as I cain."

"I'll cool him down for you." Bryce took Legs into the barn. "He'll be ready when you are."

"Thankee." Hattie's throat felt thick. "And thankee for lettin' me take him to Hawk's Fall."

"No problem," Bryce assured her.

With that settled, Hattie sped to the house. She rushed right by Logan and Miz Willow, who were playing checkers, into the storeroom. She'd need marshmallow salve to soothe the burnt skin and lady slipper tea for the pain and to help Daisy sleep. Hattie just knew she'd been up all night fretting.

The folks who'd helped put out the fire would've breathed in a lot of smoke. She'd need more of the eucalyptus and peppermint salve, along with the black cohosh and coltsfoot leaf tea. She'd bring along some stevia to sweeten the taste. Smoke had probably stung the eyes, too, so she'd need some eyebright to make a wash.

"What's wrong, Hattie?" Miz Willow leaned into the storeroom doorway.

"Fire at Daisy's place. She and Jamie got out, but she's got a burned arm and there'll be plenty of folks who need to git the smoke outta their lungs." Hattie took a deep breath. "There's nothing left, Miz Willow."

"I see." Miz Willow folded her into a hug. "Bring 'em back with you. I'll be glad to have Jamie close by. We've got plenty of room."

"Thankee, Miz Willow." Hattie's eyes filled with tears. Miz Willow had known Hattie couldn't ask her to take more people into her home, but it needed to happen. Miz Willow's big heart made room.

"I'll go with you." Logan put a hand on her arm as she went to the door. "You shouldn't be riding alone all that way."

"I've done it before." Hattie shrugged away his hand and the warmth it sent up her arm. "There's no place to sleep for the night, and another body will be an imposition. Besides, iff'n we traveled alone, tongues would wag."

"I don't care about that." Logan's eyes darkened.

"We do," Miz Willow stated. "Hattie's reputation as a woman of the Lord is needed for people to welcome her into their homes and tell of their ailments. You and Bryce'll be leaving Salt Lick Holler, but Hattie has to live with whatever people think."

"But she needs protection," Logan insisted.

"You'll jist have to settle for protectin' her reputation." Miz Willow handed Hattie her cloak. "Godspeed, child."

"I'll be back when I cain—prob'ly a couple of days." She kissed Miz Willow on the cheek and turned to Logan. "Take good care of everybody while I'm gone." She impulsively reached out to squeeze his hand. "I'm counting on you, Logan."

Logan could hardly believe it. Just that morning Hattie had been with them around the breakfast table, and in the twinkling of an eye, she was off. And she counted on him to hold down the fort while she wasn't around.

She'll only be gone for a couple of days. That's a drop in the bucket, Logan. Why are you so put out?

❧

"I don' know what happened." Daisy sniffed back tears. "Jamie crawled over to wake me up."

"He's a hero," Hattie praised, ruffling the little boy's hair. "Now you drink up this tea, and then I'll have you put some salve on yore chest. It'll holp with the coughin'. You've grown so big since I saw you last, Jamie!"

It was true. Hattie stifled a pang of guilt. Even if she'd visited more often, there wasn't much she could do aside from giving Daisy the right yarbs to make sure Jamie slept well. She surely couldn't have prevented the fire. It seemed as though a spark had jumped from the fire and lit up the hearth rug.

"He saved our lives." Daisy managed a genuine smile. "Yore my blessing, sweetheart." She went to hug him but stopped short since he was drinking the tea.

"How's yore arm feelin'?" Hattie glanced at the bandages covering Daisy's left wrist and forearm.

"Better since that salve of yores, Hattie. It holped with the stingin' after you cleaned it with that rinse you made."

"Good." Hattie would check and rebandage it in a few hours. It wasn't a pretty sight, but it hadn't gone deeper than the skin. So long as they warded off infection, Daisy would heal just fine.

"You need to put some of that salve on, too," Hattie admonished when Daisy tried to stifle a cough. "Otherwise I'll have to give you sommat stronger to clear yore lungs. I may still have to, as a matter of fact."

"Yes, ma'am." Daisy opened the jar and saw to Jamie before using it on herself. "Ooh, that is better."

"You took too much of a risk going back in." Hattie had to speak her mind. "You could've come out much worse for it."

"I know, but Jamie needs his blanket. He don't ask for

much, Hattie." Daisy's eyes glistened. "And if I didn't get my tatting shuttle and thread, we'd have no way to feed ourselves."

"I ken what you mean, Daisy." Hattie patted her good arm. "But yore more valuable than either of those things—to Jamie and to me."

"Thankee, Hattie. Yore a good sister-in-law and a better friend."

"Do you know where to go from here?" Hattie gestured around the small barn where she, Daisy, and Jamie had spent the night. Daisy's mule was the only other occupant.

"I don't know." Daisy's head drooped. "We still have a roof o'er our heads, and I've got some lace I've already made that'll see us through until I cain make more. Folks have been kind enough to drop off food and blankets they cain't really spare. I reckon I'll jist have to lean on the Lord. We'll get by."

"Shore you will," Hattie reassured. "But Miz Willow and I reckon you and Jamie should come stay with us. We've got plenty of room, and we've been wishin' for a long while now you two was closer." Hattie could see Daisy struggle with the idea for a moment.

"My pride says no, but the truth of the matter is, yore invitation is a relief." Daisy looked at her son. "I'll be glad to have Jamie in a warm home."

"Good. I'm glad that's settled." Hattie stood up. "Fact is, Miz Willow's rheumatiz is actin' up. I'd hoped it'd improve after the cold season, but she ain't doin' so well as I'd like. I'm away from home most days. I'll be glad to know yore there to keep an eye on her."

"I'd be happy to." Daisy smiled, and Hattie could see that the thought of being useful made coming to Salt Lick Holler easier on her.

"We'll head back tomorra iff'n you and Jamie aren't coughing still. For now, I'll go 'round and tend to the others." Hattie left Daisy to explain the move to Jamie. There were plenty of others with smoke in their eyes and lungs to see to.

Lord, how cain I convince Daisy to sell her land and stay with us permanently? She's already a humble woman, and I don't want to break what little pride she has left. Please prepare her heart and let the next few weeks go well. How cain I best holp Yore people, Lord?

nineteen

The answer came to Logan. After he and Bryce had talked about the money, and the conversation wandered around to the people of the holler, the way to spend the money became clear to him.

He hadn't said anything about it to anyone but Bryce, but he had high hopes. The way to help these people had been staring him in the face this whole time.

He'd written a letter to Jack Tarhill, an old friend from primer school who'd moved out to Charleston and opened an elegant shop there. He'd asked whether Jack would be interested in hand-carved nativities and checker sets or if he knew anybody who would. He also queried whether Jack had any connection with someone who used the fur pelts and skins collected around the holler by trappers. Today the reply had arrived, with good news.

Dear Logan,

Good to hear from you, buddy. Martha's doing well, and we have a brand-new baby girl. That's right. I've become a proud papa.

Finishing Touch is doing well—you wouldn't believe how many people will pay good money for trinkets and doodads that have absolutely no use. That's not to say that the things your friends make have no use—I pride myself on my checker playing. Besides, I've a healthy respect for anything that can turn a profit. Why don't you come on to Charleston and stay with me and the wife? Bring samples of the products, and we'll put them on display for two days. If they sell, I'd be happy to place an order. At any rate, it'd be good to see you.

Come over anytime—no need to write back. I hate to waste time. Hope to see you soon!

Sincerely,
Frank Tarhill

P.S. I spoke with my friend Barton Rumsford about the pelts. He's willing to pay for mink, otter, beaver, red fox, and some poor creature called the spotted skunk. I'll set up a meeting with him for you—bring a few along with you so he can check the quality.

"Whoo-ee!" Logan let out a whoop that had Bryce scrambling up the ladder.

"What?"

"Frank Tarhill wrote back. He wants to give the checkerboards and nativity sets a trial run in his store. And he has a pal who's interested in the pelts—right now the Trevors aren't getting anywhere near their value."

"Terrific." Bryce clapped him on the back. "Well, you'd better go and ask Otis, Asa, Ted, and Fred if they're game."

"Let's go!"

❧

"All right, I think that's everything." Daisy planted her hands on her hips and winced as she jarred her sore arm.

"Before we load it onto Fetch, we need to reconsider the traveling arrangements," Hattie suggested. "Since yore arm is botherin' you, you shouldn't hold Jamie and the reins. How 'bout he rides on Legs with me while you and Fetch carry yore things?"

"Good idea," Daisy agreed gratefully. "Let's load her up, then."

Together the two women situated the meager bundles that made up all Daisy and Jamie owned. The workbasket with Daisy's tatting, Jamie's blanket, and some dried meat and apples filled two saddlebags. Hattie's medicine satchel and extra supplies took up nearly the same amount of space.

They'd risen with the sun, and by the time they were ready to set out, the morning air was still chilly. Hattie saw Daisy shiver and was glad she'd thought to bring along her old cloak.

"Here, Daisy." She rummaged through a saddlebag to pull it out. It was worn and mended, but it would keep Daisy warm on the ride. Jamie would sit on Hattie's lap, and she'd wrap her cloak around him.

"Yore so good to me, Hattie." Daisy fingered the material.

"I'm jist passin' on the Lord's blessings. Lovejoy sent me this here fine new cloak, so I've no need of the other. It's old, but it'll still serve."

"I'm glad to have it." Daisy thanked her and shrugged it on. "Yore shore it's all right for me an' Jamie to come while you have visitors already?"

"Absolutely. In fact, it'll do Jamie good to meet Logan and Bryce. They're fine men. Besides, they'll be leavin' afore summer's ended." Hattie tamped down a wave of sadness. At least Logan and Bryce would still be there when she and Daisy brought Jamie home this evening.

He wouldn't be there when Hattie got home. The thought of not telling her he was going away for a while, of not seeing her before he left, sent a pang through Logan's heart. Later, when he told her why he'd had to leave, she'd understand.

If he waited for her to come home so he could say goodbye, it'd be another week before he could catch the train to Charleston. Too much was riding on this trip for him to wait to see Hattie before he left. Bryce would stay behind to keep watch over Miz Willow until Hattie got back. Besides, he'd understood Logan's need to go alone.

"Like I said before, this is your adventure." Bryce shrugged. "I'm here to help where I can, but it's your path to follow."

Otis Nye had given Logan three of the beautiful checker sets and mentioned he'd been working on chess ones, too. They weren't ready yet, though. Asa had been more than happy to send along two completed nativities. Ted and Fred danced a little jig at the thought of getting more money for the pelts they trapped and rushed to the barn to get one of every animal listed in Jack's letter.

They'd each given him their blessing and trusted him to work out the best deal he could. Logan only hoped he'd not give them reason to regret it.

"Go on, then," the old woman ordered. "I cain see yore itchin' to leave. It's sommat more important than the wandrerin' spirit that brought you here, I ken. I ain't about to keep you from followin' yore heart—'specially since you promise it'll bring you back to us!"

He hadn't felt right telling Miz Willow or anyone not already involved about the whole thing—if it failed, Otis, Asa, Fred, and Ted would already be plenty disappointed without having the whole holler know about it.

This trip was important to too many people for him to botch it up. This was a man's work, and he needed to shoulder the load. Back at Chance Ranch, he'd always been the youngest brother. The smallest, the jokester. Not the brother whom anyone would entrust with complicated business dealings or negotiations. Pretty much anything that demanded tact was delegated to someone else.

But the people of the holler saw him as a man. Asa, Otis, and the twins trusted him with their most valuable possessions and sent him to barter their skills and bring back a deal that would change their lives. Hattie entrusted to him the welfare of the holler. He wouldn't let them down. He couldn't.

He put his Bible on his lap and turned to 1 Corinthians 13. The circuit rider back home gave him the reference before he left, and now Logan wanted to read it again.

"When I was a child, I spake as a child, I understood as a child, I thought as a child: but when I became a man, I put away childish things."

There it was. God's words stood right in front of Logan. It was time to put away childish things and take on the responsibilities of a man. It was the only way he'd fulfill God's purpose for his life.

Lord, Hattie's become a dear friend to me, and I reckon she's become more important even than that. If that's Your will and part of the reason You brought me to Salt Lick Holler, then I ask You to work in her heart. Don't let her be hurt that I had to leave. You're leading me to Charleston same as You led me here, and I can only ask that You give me the focus to fulfill Your plan instead of dreaming up my own. When I return, I pray that I'll bring good news for the families of the holler, and, if it's Your will, a wedding ring.

Hattie judged it would be a long day in the saddle. Daisy's old mule was slower than usual, loaded down with more than it was accustomed to carrying. Hattie kept Legs at a sedate walk, going nowhere near as quickly as she'd galloped to Hawk's Fall.

The animals were tiring by the time the sun shone high in the sky, and Hattie figured they deserved a break. They all did. Jamie had been quiet and still almost the whole way so far, snoozing through most of the morning. She knew of a small waterfall not too far ahead.

"Hey, Daisy," Hattie called back. "Thar's water a little ways up. How 'bout we stop for some dinner?"

"Sounds good to me," Daisy agreed. "Ole Fetch here could use a drink. So could I, come to think of it."

Not long after, they sat in the shade of an old oak, munching on cheese and jerky. Jamie scooted himself to the bank of the water. Hattie started to get up.

"No." Daisy's whisper stopped her. "Let me take care of it."

"Not with yore arm as it is," Hattie refused. "I'm jist gonna sit close to him to make shore he don' fall in. He should have a little fun—he's been so good through this whole thing."

"All right." Daisy leaned back against the tree and watched as Hattie walked over to Jamie and sat down beside him.

" 'At-uh." Jamie spoke the word and gestured.

"That's right. Water." Hattie dipped a tin cup in the water and handed it to him.

" 'Ank-oo." Jamie took a sip of the water.

"Yore welcome, Jamie." Hattie slipped him a piece of cheese. "Finish yore dinner."

"Yez, Hat-ty." He ate the cheese and took a few more sips of the water. "Here." He handed her the cup so she could drink.

"Thankee, Jamie." She smiled and took a big sip before refilling the cup. "How 'bout we take this to yore mama?"

"Ma," Jamie agreed. He put his hands on the ground and started scooting toward her. Jamie would never walk on account of his palsy, but he managed to move around just the same.

Hattie stayed beside him, keeping pace with him until they reached Daisy. She handed him the cup.

"Here, Ma." He carefully gave the water to Daisy.

"Jist what I needed," Daisy said appreciatively before taking a drink.

They packed up what was left of the food and saddled up again. Hours later, they came to the fork in the road that led to Miz Willow's house.

"We're almost home," Hattie whispered to Daisy so as not to rouse Jamie. "Logan and Bryce sleep in the barn, so we'll probably wake them when we take care of the animals. I'll put Jamie in bed first."

"All right."

Hattie carried the four-year-old into the house and tucked him in bed next to Miz Willow. She and Daisy would use the pallets Miz Willow had set up on the floor. She came back out to find Bryce leading Legs to the barn.

"Woke you up that easy, did we?" Hattie couldn't hide her surprise.

"Hadn't fallen asleep yet." Bryce led Daisy and Fetch into the barn first.

"Where's Logan?" Hattie didn't see him and wondered if he was still asleep.

"He had to go," Bryce confessed. "He said to tell you he's sorry he couldn't wait for you to get back from Hawk's Fall, but the train to Charleston left last night. He'll be back in about a week, give or take a few days."

"He's gone?" Hattie asked in disbelief. She'd been at Hawk's Fall for three days, and he'd left, just like that? "Why?"

"Well. . ." Bryce shuffled uncomfortably. "It's not my place to say. He asked me to tell you he's sorry, and he'll be back as soon as he cain."

Hattie nodded as though she understood, but her thoughts roiled around in her mind as she helped unload the animals.

Why wouldn't he tell me why he was going? Did he wait until I wasn't here on purpose? I entrusted him with the holler—the people I care about. How could he have gone?

twenty

"I'll be with you in just a minute, sir—" Jack Tarhill looked up from the counter at his fancy shop, and a grin broke across his face. "Logan Chance! You got here in an awful hurry."

"Sure did." Logan smiled back. "Good to see you, Jack." He slapped his palms on the counter. "Nice place you got here." He gave a low whistle as he looked around at embroidered towels, ribbons, mirrors, pianofortes, music boxes, and the like.

"Frilly, more like." Jack shook his head. "But it keeps me in business. Speaking of which, I'm supposed to meet Barton Rumsford for dinner in about ten minutes. I was just about to leave. Why don't you come along?"

"If there's food, you can count me in." Logan's stomach rumbled, showing the truth in his words.

"I see." Jack laughed. "Well, let's go get that hollow leg of yours filled up."

An hour later, Logan groaned. "I can't put away another bite."

"Good," Barton Rumsfeld proclaimed. "Now we can get down to business."

"Fine by me." Logan liked Bart—he was a short man with a big laugh and the belly to match it.

"Let's go to my store, and Logan'll set out the things he brought in the back room," Jack suggested. "I need to be getting back."

About twenty minutes later, Logan unwrapped the bundle of furs and displayed them on a large flat table Jack said he used for products coming in and out of the store. Bart didn't say a word until he looked over each fur carefully, front and back.

"Good stuff," he decided aloud. "Skinned well, no bald spots. Clean, too."

"These are the types of pelts Jack mentioned in his letter," Logan explained, "but the Trevor twins also have the occasional white-tailed deer or bear hide. Lots of rabbits, too."

"I have all the rabbit fur I need. It's pretty common these days." Bard stroked his full beard. "The deer and bear might come in useful. If they have it, they can telegram ahead before they send it so I'll know if I've a place for it."

"So you're interested in setting up a deal?" Logan didn't press too hard but moved the meeting along.

"Yep. Otter and beaver skins are always in demand, and right now mink's all the rage for ladies' coats." Bart thought aloud. "I've got a friend who's using the spotted skunk skins. 'Course, that's on the basis that the quality is still high."

He started listing what he could pay per pelt depending on the size and type of animal. Logan nodded solemnly and accepted the terms. Bart offered more than twice what the Trevor twins were already getting. Logan would celebrate the good news later—for now, he didn't want Bart to lower his price.

"Sounds reasonable. I'll run it past the Trevors. They do pretty well, but I will tell you they stop trapping for a particular animal when the numbers get low."

"Smart boys." Bart nodded wisely. "Does no good to get them all at once, or there won't be any next time around. Can't tell you how many times that's happened. Awful thing." He stood up and held out his hand. "Let's shake on it."

Logan was more than happy to oblige. When Bart left, he took the furs with him and left money behind. Logan would go back to the holler with at least one family taken care of. Now for the others. He walked out onto the shop floor and waited while Jack helped a customer buy a gilded frame.

"Now that I've got a minute," Jack said as the woman left, "why don't we take a look at what you brought for me?"

This time, Logan simply set out the boxes and let Jack unwrap the carvings inside, let him feel the smooth texture of the wood, notice the fine detail for himself as he uncovered each piece. The products would speak for themselves.

"Well, now." Jack gave a low whistle as he looked at the entire nativity spread out before him. "That'll make a fine display. Fine craftsmanship."

"The best," Logan agreed.

"Hold up a minute while I put it out." Logan helped Jack carry the pieces out to a prominent display area and watched his friend expertly set them up.

Logan sucked in a sharp breath when he saw the figure Jack wrote on the price tag. It was a lot of money. But Jack's store did quite well in Charleston. He'd know better about fine art than Logan did.

They went back to the table and opened up the checker sets. Jack ran his hand along the board, testing its weight and the smoothness of its surface before picking up the checkers and turning them over in his hands. "Good size. Perfect shape. The staining on the wood is even and precise." Jack squinted at the bottom of a checker. "He's even carved circles on the bottom of each piece! And that's nothing compared to the clean lines of the crown on the top."

They both heard a bell, and Jack walked out to help the customer. Logan finished unpacking all of the round checkers and set them up as though ready for a game. Jack came back in, smiling from ear to ear.

"Guess what just sold?"

❧

He'd been gone for five days. Hattie could scarcely believe how much she missed Logan Chance.

Good thing he took off now so's I'll be prepared for when he leaves for good. I knew from the git-go he weren't goin' to stay. So I'll stop pining like some young maid after her beau. Logan's not my beau, and it's wrong of me to have let my feelings go so deep. Besides, he up and left without a word. He didn't even explain to Miz Willow where he was goin'. It's that scamp in him that's made him hie off. Best I realize that now, so I don't make a fool of myself when he comes back.

Hattie had told herself the same thing every day since she'd brought Daisy and Jamie back to Salt Lick Holler and found out Logan had gallivanted off. She had no business missing him—it wasn't as though he was missing her. She beat the rug with more force than she meant to, sending a cloud of dust into her face.

See? If that ain't proof yore notions about Logan Chance are clouding yore vision, nothin' will be.

She heard a heavy pounding on the door and walked around to the front of the house to find out who was causing the ruckus. She tried to ignore the flutter of hope that Logan had come back, but her heart clenched when she saw Nate Rucker instead.

"It's time, Hattie!" Nate grabbed hold of her shoulder with one powerful hand and scooted her through the door Daisy had opened. His eyes were wide and frantic. "Abigail's havin' the babe!"

❧

"It's all right, Abby," Miz Willow crooned. "Breathe in and out, long and slow. That's it. The cramps'll let up in jist a minute."

"Hoo." Abigail let out a shaky breath, her eyes screwed tightly shut. "Ooh." She fell back against the chair as the pangs subsided. "That one were powerful fierce."

"You've got a bit afore the next one will come on." Hattie

laid clean towels on the bed before pulling up the sheets and laying more towels for good measure. She went to the kettle to pour some motherwort tea.

Abigail sipped some of it before handing the mug back. "I'd like to walk a bit."

"Whatever makes you more comfortable," Miz Willow agreed.

"I've given up on comfortable," Abigail gritted out before doubling over with another onset of cramps.

"Yore doin' jist fine." Hattie held Abigail's arm to support her. "Think on yore precious babe. Yore gonna make a fine mother, Abby."

"I hope so." Abigail straightened up and paced around the cabin, letting gravity do its work.

"I know so," Miz Willow declared. Awhile later, Abigail's cramps were coming on much faster. She'd been in labor for nearly nine hours.

"I reckon it's time we git you to the bed, Abby." Hattie helped Abigail out of the rocking chair and winced at how tightly Abby clenched her hand as a spasm rocked her body. "Won't be long now."

"It's already been long enough," Abby moaned as she was put in bed. "Did Nate bring the ax?"

"Yes, Abby. It's under yore bed already to holp cut the pain." Hattie didn't know exactly how having an ax under the bed would help, but the thought seemed to comfort women in labor.

"Now, Abby," Miz Willow instructed after she examined the woman, "when the next one comes, I want you to push. Do you hear me?"

"Yes." Abby gritted her teeth and bore down immediately. The pain lasted longer, but the babe hadn't come yet.

"Now keep on pushing as hard as you cain every time you

git the urge." Hattie mopped Abby's brow as she spoke.

About an hour later, Abigail's strength was flagging. "I don't think I cain push anymore," she wailed, tears trailing down her cheeks and splashing onto her nightgown.

"Shore you cain, honey!" Li'l Nate roared his encouragement through the shut door. From the sound of it, he'd been pacing back and forth the whole time, letting out groans when Abby yelled with the pain.

"You don't know what yore talkin' 'bout, Nathaniel Rucker." Abigail sat up and bellowed back. "Jist hobble yore mouth!"

"Yes, dear." Nate obeyed meekly. Hattie heard the sound of his boots as he started pacing again.

"One more time, Abby," Hattie encouraged. "Push as hard as you cain and don't stop until we say."

"AAARRRGGGH!" Abigail hollered as she pushed through the pain. The babe's cry hovered in the air.

A few minutes later, Abigail leaned back against the pillows, panting from exertion, her eyes closed. She smiled when Hattie laid the baby in her arms.

"I'm comin' in!" Nate pounded on the door.

"No yore not, Nate. You know the rule. New father waits half an hour before comin' in." Miz Willow's dictum gave the midwives enough time to clean up the mother and the baby and gave the woman some time to rest up before her man saw her. Only then would he find out whether he'd been given a son or daughter. That was the mother's news to tell.

Abigail will fill my old home with love and laughter and children, Hattie thought. *It's only right to celebrate that. I won't think about how I never had the joy of telling my husband I'd given him a baby lad or lass. 'Twasn't to be so and never will be.*

twenty-one

Logan stood at the counter of the biggest mercantile he'd ever seen. He'd been walking around the place for almost an hour now. The checker sets and nativities had sold in the two days, and Jack had ordered more. Logan would be coming back with good news for Otis, Asa, and the twins. But first he needed to pick up a few things to help get them going.

"What've you got here?" The proprietor wheezed and rubbed his hands together, like he was counting his money in his mind before Logan even gave it to him.

"Two whittling knives, one extra-large leather apron, four traps, a bolt of blue cotton, two cans of varnish, and a sack of peppermint sticks." Logan looked at the items and checked the list he and Bryce had thought up.

Asa and Otis would get a knife and can of varnish each. Li'l Nate needed a bigger leather apron, and the traps would go to the Trevor twins. He'd added the peppermint sticks for Hattie—she liked to use them to stir her tea. He figured that Hattie's friend whose house had burned down could put the fabric to good use. That made him think of all the things Lovejoy and the women had bought back in Reliable.

"Can I get a comb, a brush, a pack of needles, and a few spools of your finest thread in white, black, and blue?" Logan knew he probably hadn't thought of everything, but it was the best he could do at the moment.

"Sure. Anything else?"

"Yeah." Logan took a deep breath. "Do you carry wedding rings?"

Two hours later he sat in yet another train car, heading back to Salt Lick Holler. He kept sticking his hand in his shirtfront pocket to finger the small gold band inside, making sure it was still there. In a matter of days, he'd be back in Salt Lick Holler, where he could get down on one knee and ask Hattie to become his bride.

❧

"I'm home!" Logan all but shouted it through the front door.

No, you're not, Logan Chance. This isn't yore real home, and I have to remember it even if you don't.

"Well, git on in here so we cain see iff'n you still look the same!" Miz Willow called back.

Hattie had forgotten how tall he was until he had to stoop a little to get through the doorway. Had he been so handsome and dynamic the last time she saw him? Surely not. Hattie grabbed the fennel seed tea she'd put together for Abigail Rucker. It would help her milk to come after yesterday's birthing.

"Hello, Hattie." The nerve of that man to smile at her like that after he'd up and left without a word of explanation! No scapegrace smile was going to make up for his leaving her and abandoning the people she'd entrusted to him.

"Welcome back, Logan." She gave him a perfunctory smile. "Miz Willow will introduce you to Daisy and Jamie while I run over to the Ruckers'. Abigail delivered her son yesterday." She slipped through the door without waiting for anyone to stop her.

She all but stomped in her frustration as she made her way to Abigail's home. It wasn't as though she'd expected him to frown when he got back, but to smile as though all was right in the world was too much.

That's not what's really upsetting me, she admitted to herself. *Even after what he did, after he let me down for a pleasure trip to Charleston, I still responded to his smile. It warmed me clear down to my toes before I pulled myself together. Logan Chance is downright dangerous. How could I have forgotten how charming he is? I'll have to guard myself against him until he leaves for good.*

Hattie ignored the sharp pang in her chest at the thought. *I'm jist winded. I've been walking so fast. That's all. Nothing more.* She could already see the Rucker place! Hattie took a calming breath before knocking on the door and giving Nate the tea. She stayed to chat with Abby and make sure everything was going well.

"He's sleepin' awful deep. Not very hungry," the new mother said worriedly.

"That's normal. It usually takes a day or so, Abby," Hattie reassured her. "I brung you some fennel seed tea to holp you make plenty of milk."

"Thankee, Hattie." Abigail turned to Nate. "Nate, let Hattie hold Bitty Nate." She smiled happily. "His papa will hardly put him down for a minute."

"That's right." Nate cuddled his son close for a second before carefully handing him to Hattie.

She nestled the tiny babe close to her heart. He smelled like just-dried laundry and newness. His tiny hands and even tinier fingernails were perfect and pink and clean. Dark swirls of hair wisped over the top of his head, and he let out a big yawn from his tiny mouth before dropping off to sleep.

Hattie cherished the moment, snuggling close to the baby and feeling his warm weight in her arms. She'd never have a babe of her own, but she'd been a part of bringing this precious child into the world yesterday. It was enough. It had to be.

❧

Logan waited for Hattie to come back from the Rucker place. He'd walked a ways up so they'd be able to talk in private, but he wasn't sure how well the meeting was going to go.

She didn't seem glad to see me. Why did she leave the second I got back, like she couldn't stand to be in the same room as me? Is she nursing the grievance that I left? Did it hurt her so badly? Wouldn't that mean she cared for me, if she missed me that much? Will she let me make it up to her?

The questions flooded his mind as he held the ring, warming it in his hands while he waited for Hattie to walk down the road—hopefully into his arms. If felt as though he'd waited for months when he finally saw her coming along the path. She stopped for a moment when she caught sight of him, and something flickered across her face before she kept walking.

"I've been waiting for you, Hattie." Logan's voice sounded gruff to his own ears, but the words had a double meaning. He hadn't just waited for her today by the side of the road—he'd been waiting to love her for his entire life.

"I cain see that." Hattie didn't look at him, and she kept walking.

"Hey, hold up a minute!" He fell into step beside her. "There's something I need to talk with you about."

"Right now?"

"Yes. Now." He guided her over to a fallen log so they could sit down. "Why are you trying to get away from me, Hattie?"

"I. . ." She sighed. "Why don't you say what you have to say, Logan?"

"I know you don't understand why I left," he began.

"No, I don't," she stated flatly.

"And I can't tell you yet," Logan continued.

"I didn't ask you to."

"It's a matter of honor," he tried to explain. "I can't tell you until I've told the others first. I gave my word."

"And what of yore promise to me, Logan?" She spoke the question softly, but it demanded an answer. "I entrusted you with the holler while I was away."

"Hattie." He took her hands in his. "You have to believe me. I didn't leave *from* the holler. I left *for* the holler. I can see now that my leaving hurt you, Hattie." He looked into her eyes. "I'm sorry for that."

"You couldn't have waited one day?" The small whisper nearly broke his heart.

"No. It would have meant waiting for more than a week. I had to follow through with my responsibilities."

"Fine, Logan." She tried to stand up, but he held on tight.

"I came back to you, Hattie." Silently he begged for her to understand. "I love you. I want you to become my wife." He brought out the ring and tried to slide it onto her finger.

"No!" She pushed him away. "I cared for you. I trusted you to keep yore word to me, to take care of the others I love. Instead, you went hieing off to Charleston. I cain't give my hand and heart to a man who gallivants off whenever the notion takes him." She wiped furiously at her tears. "You spoke of responsibilities. I have many. Even if I did trust that you wouldn't take off and leave me, I cain't marry you and leave my people."

"Hattie!" He tried to stop her, but she ran off. He sank down onto the log.

How did I mess everything up so badly? How can she think I would willingly hurt her and abandon the people she loves? Should I explain myself, or is this Your answer, Lord? I can't wed a woman who doesn't trust me. I thought Hattie and I shared something special. Where do we go from here, Lord? I love her.

❧

Hattie ran until she had no more breath and sank down underneath a white pine, sobs wracking her body.

He wants to marry me, and I said no! I love him, and still I said no! Lord, I cain't leave the holler. I know the work and purpose You've given me. But I ache, Jesus. I love him, but I cain't rely on him. He's not grown enough to truly understand responsibility. I cain't wed a boy with a wandering spirit and a charming smile. How soon would that smile fade and take him away forever—especially when he found out I'd bear him no children?

Father, I've done my level best to make peace and be content with what You give me. Why do You put temptation in my path? Why put this love in my heart if I cain't do anything about it? I yearn for a family, Lord. Why am I to be denied a husband? My first marriage held precious little love, and here a man is promising to care for me. And I love him, too. Why do I love the one man who will leave me or force me to leave the place You've given me? I don't understand, but I'm trying so hard to follow Yore will. I love him, but it cain never be. Why?

She whispered again in a broken sob that carried away on the wind, "Why?"

twenty-two

"So how'd it go?" Bryce asked later that night as they were heading back to the barn.

Worse than I ever could have imagined. Logan realized there was no possible way Bryce could know he'd proposed to Hattie—and been rejected.

"What?" He shook his head to clear it.

"Charleston? Frank Tarhill?" Bryce looked at him strangely. "You know, the whole trip. You took off for a walk right after you got back, so you haven't told me what happened."

"It went well." Logan managed a smile at the thought of telling the guys tomorrow. "Frank wants more checker sets and nativities. Bart will take the furs on an ongoing basis for an appreciable fee increase. I also got everything on the list so they could get started. Frank and Bart already paid me for the first installment."

"That's the best news I've heard all week." Bryce grinned. "Do we get to tell everybody tomorrow?"

Logan thought about how upset he'd made Hattie that evening. It'd be a good idea to give her some space and give them both time to think. He nodded at Bryce.

The next morning they set out to see Otis Nye. They found him squinting at a carved owl, which was squinting right back.

"If you're in the middle of a staring contest, I have to tell you, Otis, I don't think you're going to win." Bryce grinned as he said it.

"Listen up, whippersnapper," Otis growled. "I could outstare you anytime, anyplace."

"I'll have to take you up on that someday." Bryce laughed. "But for now, Logan here came to talk business."

"Oh?" Otis raised one scraggly white eyebrow.

"How many of those checkerboards do you think you can make, Otis?"

"I'll be." A smile broke out across the old man's craggy face.

"This is your cut for the first two—they both already sold." Logan handed him a small bag.

Otis opened it with shaky hands, and his mouth dropped open in disbelief. He peered at Logan suspiciously.

"What are you tryin' to pull?" He pulled himself up and flung the bag back at Logan. "You tryin' to make me a charity case? Git out."

"No." Logan tossed the bag back. "Take that, divide it by two. That's how much you get for every checkerboard that you make and Frank Tarhill sells. He's getting just as much profit as you are—more, in fact, since you put in all the time. He'll pay for the freight costs."

"Glory be." The old man turned the coins over in his blue-veined hands. "Thankee, Logan Chance. You, too, Bryce. You tell that Frank fella he jist has to tell me how many he needs."

After giving Otis his new whittling knife and a can of varnish, Logan and Bryce took their leave. They still had to visit the Pleasants and the Trevors. They came across Asa first.

"Mornin', Asa." Logan tried to sound happy in spite of his busted heart.

"Good to see you, Logan. Bryce." Asa gestured for them to come closer. "What's the word?" Cautious hope flickered in the man's eyes as Logan and Bryce grinned at him.

"Frank Tarhill's customers loved the nativities. He sold two in three days and had another woman come in asking after them." Logan handed him his money. "She paid in advance, so you've already got an order to fill. This is your share of the profits off the three sets."

"You wouldn't be pulling my leg, would you, boys?" Asa looked at the cash in shock.

"Nope." Logan clapped him on the back. "Frank wants to know how many you can make per month and still have them be of the same quality."

"I don't know." Asa shook his head in disbelief. "It were jist a hobby afore. He wants more? At this price?"

"That's right. Frank thinks they'll sell particularly well around Christmas, so he wants you to be ready to fill a big order by winter." Logan grinned. "He says that since you put in all the work for half the profit, he'll pay for the freight costs."

"By the way," Bryce added, "Otis Nye carves mighty fine checkerboards. Frank's put in an order for those, too." He handed Asa another whittling knife and can of varnish, just as they'd given to Otis. "We figure you two might keep each other company while you work sometime."

"Thankee." Asa still looked stunned. "I'll be shore to do that."

When they got to the Trevor place, Ted and Fred took one look at their grins and started whooping.

"Good news is a-comin'—I cain tell by the look on yore faces." Ted, Logan guessed, gave an excited jump.

"Like the cat with a saucer of cream," Fred agreed.

"You're right." Logan handed them their money and started going over the prices Bart Rumsford was willing to pay for the various pelts.

"No foolin'?" Their jaws hung open.

"No fooling," Bryce repeated, then handed them their package. "So we thought you could use a few more traps."

"You boys come on with us to put them out," they insisted.

In no rush to get back to the healers' place, Logan decided to go along. Bryce came, too. They made their way around the hills to the places where the twins promised they'd had the most success this time of year.

On their way back for something to eat, they heard someone yell. A single gunshot followed. Without a word, all four men raced in the direction of the noise. The closer they got, the more screams they heard.

❧

Hattie scrubbed at a spot on her yellow dress, rattling the washboard. She welcomed the hard work—it gave her hands something to do and her head something to focus on besides Logan. He and Bryce had started off right after breakfast, during which Logan hadn't said but two words.

The strong fumes of the lye stung her eyes and nose. She sniffed and blinked back tears as she took the now-clean dress over to the rinsing water, but even without the lye, she had a hard time stopping the tears.

Is this the way it has to be now? We cain't even be at the same table? There'll be no more shared laughter or smiles so long as this keeps up—and even fewer onc' he's gone for good.

"Hattie!" Logan came charging up on an unfamiliar horse.

"Not now, Logan." She bent over the laundry and surreptitiously dried her eyes.

"Now, Hattie." Logan's tone brooked no argument. "Get your satchel while I saddle up Legs. Rooster stumbled into a bear trap and shot himself in the foot, trying to get free."

Hattie sprung into action, running to the storeroom and pulling down anything she thought she could possibly use. She grabbed the entire bolt of clean white gauze Lovejoy had sent, along with every cleanser and calming powder she could lay a hand to. Every yarb known to stop blood flow found its way into a bag.

She had tweezers and a magnifying glass in her satchel. The most she'd ever used them for was a splinter, but today they'd be needed for much more. Needles and strong thread lay at the ready. She grabbed clean bandages and her cloak and headed out the door. Logan already stood there with Legs. She tied her bags to the saddle, and he lifted her up. She refused to dwell on the warmth of his hands on her waist. Now wasn't the time to think of such things.

They galloped all the way to the Linden place, and Hattie could hear the yells for half a mile before they got there. A bloody makeshift stretcher lay outside the door. Hattie rushed past it to get inside.

Nessie was pressed against the far wall, her hands over her mouth as she watched her father fight Bryce and the Trevor boys. He shouted nonsense about how they all wanted to kill him. The moment Hattie drew near, she could detect the odor of moonshine underlying the smell of blood.

"He passed out while we carried him," Bryce grunted, trying to hold Rooster down. "But he came to not long ago and won't lie still. He's making the bleeding worse."

She looked at the blood-soaked sheets around Rooster's mangled leg and knew there wasn't a moment to lose. As quickly as she could, Hattie doused a rag with ether and held it against Rooster's nose and mouth. He looked at her with wild eyes and clawed at her arms before he passed out.

"Nessie, I need you to get some strong rope—as much of it as you cain find." Hattie rolled up her sleeves. "I'm going to need you boys to tie him down. Even unconscious, he'll jerk around while I try to staunch the bleeding and clean his wounds. I'll have to find and remove the bullet if it didn't pass clean through."

Hattie applied pressure to the leg to stop the bleeding. The bottom half of Rooster's right shin was shredded from the teeth of the trap and looked to be fractured in at least two places.

His foot was in slightly better shape. "Looks like the bullet shot straight through the side of his instep."

"Lucky shot iff'n ever there was one," Ted thought aloud.

"God was merciful," Logan murmured.

His opinion took Hattie by surprise. Most folks would think Rooster deserved this; Logan's compassion for a drunk made her glad of his help. A sickbed ought to be a place of healing, not of judgment.

"Leg's busted up, Hattie," Logan observed.

"It's too swoll up to set. I'll have to tend the wounds for now. In a day or two, I'll need to set and splint it." Hattie cleaned the wounds with water before applying a witch hazel wash. Then she brought out the needle to stitch up the deep gashes along his leg. He'd obviously tried to yank himself free of the trap.

Hours later she wrapped the leg in bandages and sat back. Rooster slept fitfully but couldn't move enough to hurt his leg. "Breathing looks fairly steady," Logan judged.

"Iff'n we cain keep the wounds from festerin' and set them bones, might be he gets through jist fine," she replied. She looked Logan in the eye before delivering her warning. "The real trouble will come when he wakes up."

twenty-three

"Nessie," Hattie said, "you go tell Miz Willow what's happenin'. She's been at the Ruckers' today. And take yore nightdress. I want you to stay the night and holp Daisy with Miz Willow and Jamie." Hattie tried her best to keep Nessie away from the worst of Rooster's treatment. Logan suspected if the young woman stayed, Hattie would have another patient.

Logan took his cue from her. "Ted, Fred, you were a great help. I think we have things under control here now."

They looked to Hattie, who nodded her approval.

"We'll walk Nessie on o'er to Miz Willow," Ted said. They took their leave.

Hattie spent the next hours pouring water down Rooster's throat, though he mostly slept through the night. It must have been the combination of the moonshine he'd so obviously been drinking before the accident, the ether she'd used before looking at the wound, the intense pain he suffered, and the lady slipper root tea she trickled into his mouth. Whatever the reason, Rooster slept.

Hattie sat for a while in a straight-back chair, her knees drawn up to her chest as she watched Rooster fight off some unknown demon in his dreams. She closed her eyes. When she opened them again, Logan was looking at her.

"Go lie down, Hattie." He spoke softly so as not to wake Bryce. "I'm watching him. You need to sleep—you've done the best you can for Rooster. I'll wake you if anything changes."

Too tired to argue, Hattie nodded gratefully. "You done

good tonight. I couldn't of done this without yore holp."

"We'll keep watch, Hattie. You sleep."

"You'll wake me?" she asked again.

"You can count on me."

❧

Hattie collapsed onto the pallet and fell asleep immediately. Logan watched her. She seemed so peaceful, so fragile for the work she did. He and the Trevors had been all but certain the leg would have to be amputated, but she'd worked for hours to save it. Even now, tuckered out as she was, she somehow found the strength to get up every hour or so to check Rooster's bandages and pour some kind of tea down his throat. Logan guessed the tea was to help the man sleep.

"I cain't marry you and leave my people."

Her words from the night before echoed in his mind. She was right. He hadn't thought about what he was asking of her. How could he have imagined that the woman who cared so deeply about everyone around her—the woman he'd fallen in love with—would leave them without a healer?

Logan saw Rooster's eyelids flicker and went to wake Hattie up. When she first opened her eyes, the soft smile that spread across her face melted his heart. Then it faded. She sat up quickly.

"How is he?" She rushed over to the bed.

"I think he's coming around." Logan moved to stand at her side.

Hattie felt Rooster's forehead with her hand and frowned. "He's hot. I'll give him something for the fever along with the calming powder. The longer he sleeps, the better." She bustled over to the fire and started brewing the tea before returning to check Rooster's leg.

"How does it look?" Logan held his breath while he waited

for the answer. The thought that Rooster might lose his leg was bad enough without the knowledge of how hard Hattie had worked to avoid that very thing.

"Like he tangled with a bear trap." Hattie began dabbing at the wounds with something. "It's bad, but so long as we keep infection away, he has a chance. The other problem is that I cain't splint it much beyond the knee, so although he cain't bend the leg, he cain still move around a bit. If the bones don't set to heal over the fractures, he'll never walk on it again, no matter what else I manage to do. I'll be able to apply a splint better in a few days, onc't the swellin' goes down, but for now I'll have to watch him."

"Bryce and I will help you," Logan offered. "Nessie will be back during the day."

"I know. But it's not jist his leg we'll be dealing with, Logan." She sounded as though she were girding for battle.

"Oh?"

"While he's healing, he cain't drink. He don't have the strength to fight the headaches and the vomiting after he's been drunk," she explained. "He has to keep down enough to holp him heal."

"He can't move, so he doesn't have much of a choice," Logan reasoned. Still, Rooster would be hurting badly for want of a drink. It wouldn't be a pretty sight.

"I've brung everything I cain to holp with him wanting likker." She gestured toward the bags lying around the room. "But you cain be shore he'll try to get up and get to it any way he cain—even if it means he'll never walk again. Moonshine's got that strong a hold on him. He'll need watchin' 'round the clock." She looked at him with tired eyes. "If he pulls through this, it'll have to be body and soul. It ain't jist his leg that needs healing, Logan."

"I'm here, Hattie." Logan could only hope she heard him

with her heart and not just her ears. "I'm here."

❧

The days melted into each other, each as difficult as the last. Hattie hardly stepped foot out of Rooster's cabin. She slept in snatches on Nessie's pallet while Logan and Bryce took turns watching Rooster. Some nights she couldn't sleep until she poured enough calming tea down Rooster's throat to make him sleep first.

He slipped in and out of consciousness, alternating between fevers and chills, his body sweating out the poisons he'd been guzzling far too long. He twisted and turned, yelled and cussed, begged and pleaded for a drink. He brought up almost every drop Hattie managed to get down into him.

Many times he shouted in his delirium, calling for people who'd long left this world or breaking into off-key snatches of songs. There was nothing she could do but keep pouring various medicines down his throat to help with the nausea, headache, fevers, and pain. Eventually she was able to splint his leg fully, the fear of swelling and renewed bleeding subsiding with time and treatment.

Through it all, Logan never left Hattie's side. Regardless of the blood, sweat, yells, and never-ending mess, he stuck with her.

"Rooster, no talking like that. Miz Hattie's a lady. Here, I'll help you." Time and again, Logan stepped in. He never once lost his temper—which stunned her. She still recalled his smoldering anger the first day he'd met Rooster. Now he showed firm resolve mixed with Christian mercy and abiding respect in dealing with the man.

Often Logan escorted Hattie to the door and gently nudged her outside when it came to basic or messy matters. "I'll take care of it, Hattie." He was her anchor in the storm, strong and protective, making sure she got enough sleep and food so she could continue.

I wouldn't have gotten this far with anybody else.

The realization of how much she needed Logan shook her to the core. She didn't have time to look at it too deeply, but Hattie knew that when all of this was over, she'd still have to face a future without Logan Chance.

Hattie amazed him. Through the entire week and more, she'd relentlessly fought to save Rooster Linden from himself. She'd held the man's hand as he cried for liquor, gave him calming tea when he swore and thrashed against his constraints, filling the air with words the likes of which Logan would never want any woman to hear. Hattie returned Rooster's curses with prayers.

She slept little, grabbing catnaps when Rooster wore himself out. Curls sprang free from Hattie's loosened braid to hang around a pale face. Dark circles beneath her eyes tattled about how weary she'd grown, yet her dignity and determination never waned. Logan had never seen a woman so beautiful.

Then, as suddenly as the gunshot had gone off and started the whole ordeal, the storm began to ebb. Rooster's eyes, no longer lit with the manic need for moonshine, darkened in pain. He stopped yelling, stopped trying to get to his still, and lay quiet for hours on end. Logan and Hattie couldn't tell whether he was lost in the pain or his thoughts—probably both.

"Go home, Hattie." Logan put his hands on her arms and looked into her eyes. They looked tired but carried the first flickering of victory.

She shook her head wordlessly.

"Listen to me," he demanded. "You've held off the infection, nursed him through the fevers, and took the abuse he rained upon you. That's all over now. You've splinted his leg, and he's no longer thrashing, so he won't hurt it further. Bryce will help me watch him through the afternoon and night. You need to go home and sleep."

"I. . ." She closed her eyes, thinking it over. Determined, she raised her chin before proclaiming her decision. "I'll be back come mornin' tomorra." Her face softened as she looked at him. "Thankee, Logan."

He bundled her up in her cloak, even though the sun shone outside, and had Nessie ride with her back to Miz Willow's house before she could change her mind.

So many people had worked alongside them. Nessie had come every day to bring more medicine, mop her father's brow, and help keep the cabin as clean as possible. Bryce stayed every night, holding Rooster down when he thrashed violently against his restraints, taking turns staying up at night, and caring for the animals in the barn. The Trevor twins came to help muck out the barn every morning. Since Rooster had stepped in one of their traps, they felt partially responsible.

Silk Trevor, Miz Willow, and Mary Pleasant took turns cooking and bringing by breakfast, dinner, and supper. They also carried out the towels and bandages every day, washed them, and brought them back to be dirtied again. The entire holler banded together once they heard what was happening and looked to Logan to tell them what they could do and how Rooster was progressing. Everyone prayed.

"Logan, is Rooster sleeping?" Bryce stuck his head through the doorway.

"Yep."

"Then we need you to come outside," Bryce ordered. "Asa has gathered together the men of the holler, and they say we have a decision to make."

What is going on now? Logan walked to the door and found

a crowd waiting in the yard.

"Glad yore here, Logan." Asa stepped beside him and clapped him on the shoulder. "We're having a town vote, and you and yore brother have more than earned a say in the matter."

The men nodded and gave a general rumble of agreement before they all headed for the barn. Logan had an inkling of what this was all about.

"Here's the thing," Asa continued, once they were out of Rooster's earshot. "We don't hold with laying a hand to the property of another man, but this here is whatcha call a unique circumstance."

"Rooster coulda shot anybody," Edward Trevor growled.

"He's become a danger to the holler!" someone else shouted.

"So we're fixin' to dismantle the still." Asa opened the barn door and pointed to the far wall.

"Everybody in favor?"

Logan looked at Bryce as they both raised their hands.

"Aye!"

twenty-four

Logan helped with the most rigorous part of the work, then needed to check on Rooster. When he stepped into the cabin, he found Rooster's eyes wide open.

"Hey, Rooster," Logan spoke softly, not certain how the man would react.

"Hey, Logan." He took a deep breath. "I've a favor to ask you, though I've no right."

Lord, please don't let him ask for moonshine. Not after all Hattie's gone through. Don't let him backslide. Please.

"What is it, Rooster?" Logan pulled a chair next to the bed and sat down.

"I been doin' a lot of thinkin'," Rooster began. A rueful smile stretched across his face. "Ain't been much else to do these days. Fact is, I need to git the thoughts outta my head and into the air—see iff'n my good intentions cain live in the world."

Can it be? Has Rooster decided to turn over a new leaf? Logan nodded his encouragement.

"So I need you to do two things. First is, untie me. Now don't go shakin' yore head already," Rooster pleaded. "Listen, I'm not goin' to try and git outta bed. I ain't gonna ask for a drink or even try to git one m'self. I jist want to sit up and talk, man to man. I ain't been upright for a long while, Logan."

Something in Rooster's eyes convinced Logan. He understood the deeper meaning behind the man's words. If there was even a chance that Rooster wanted to leave liquor and come back to God, Logan could do nothing less than listen and support him. He undid the knots holding Rooster down and helped him carefully slide up and lean back on a mound of blankets. Rooster kept his word and didn't try to get up.

"Thankee, Logan." Rooster took a deep breath. "Fer everything. I cain't remember much of this week, but I know it ain't been easy on either of us. I owe you more'n I cain say."

"You don't owe me a thing, Rooster." Logan looked into his eyes. "But you do owe it to yourself and Nessie and Hattie to take better care of yourself."

"I ken what you mean, son." Rooster closed his eyes. "I stepped off the path a long while ago and lost my way. I ain't been able to see straight in a good long while."

"I know." Logan took a deep breath and plunged ahead. "Isaiah tells us of men of God who 'are swallowed up of wine, they are out of the way through strong drink; they err in vision, they stumble in judgment.'"

"That's it, right there." Rooster bowed his head. "Moonshine. It'd be easy to lay the blame on the drink, but I allowed myself to let it destroy me."

"You aren't destroyed, Rooster. You're alive, and you haven't had a drop in over a week." Logan saw the need to encourage him. "Your leg is in a bad way, but Hattie has it on the mend. You have a chance to make things right."

"That's what I want to do." Rooster's eyes filled with the depth of his emotion. "I cain decide niver to touch the stuff agin, but I don't know how to make right what I already done."

"You can't change the past, Rooster," Logan told him. "But the good news is, you don't have to. Remember 1 John 1:9? 'If we confess our sins, he is faithful and just to forgive us our sins, and to cleanse us from all unrighteousness.' Sounds to me like you're confessing and want to make a change."

"I do." Rooster began to cry. "Lord, forgive me for what I done. Holp me not to do it agin. Holp me to make it right with the people I love."

Logan prayed as he held the old man, who cried away the years he'd drowned his soul with liquor. After a while, Rooster's sobs subsided, and his drained face shone with peace.

"You know, I'll need to take down m' still," he mused, sinking down onto the bed and closing his eyes.

"I'm glad you mentioned it." Logan grinned as Rooster began to snore.

❧

Hattie woke up late the next morning to the smell of bacon frying. For the first time in more than a week, her eyes didn't feel as if a fistful of grit had blown in them. She stretched and got out of bed, pulling on her blue cotton dress. She needed to get back to Rooster.

"Oh, no you don't." Miz Willow's voice stopped her in her tracks. "You jist sit yore pretty little self down at that thar table and eat. Yore nothin' but skin an' bones."

Hattie obediently sat down and buttered a roll, suddenly realizing how hungry she was. She'd have to bring some of this back for Logan and Bryce.

"Things shore been changing 'round the holler since Logan left for Charleston." Miz Willow poured herself a cup of tea and lowered herself into the rocker.

Yep. He left without saying a word, come back with no explanation, and then proposed as though nothing had happened. How cain you expect that I'd deem him worthy of my trust anymore? I placed you and ev'rybody I love in his hands, and he let y'all slip through his fingers when he wanted to go off on another adventure. He acted like an overgrown boy.

Hattie pushed away her plate, her appetite gone.

"Otis Nye came by an' tole me all about it." Miz Willow's head bobbed up and down. "Now I ken why Logan couldn't tell us 'til after he talked to Otis, Asa, and the Trevor twins."

"What do you mean?" Hattie had no idea what her friend was going on about.

"You've been with him all week tending to Rooster, and it never came up?" Miz Willow stopped rocking. "Dearie, Logan went to Charleston on business. He done met up with an old friend and struck up a few deals. Otis has a standin' order for his fancy checker sets, and so does Asa for those nativities of his. Logan even found a new buyer for the pelts the Trevor boys trap—all at a very tidy profit."

Hattie couldn't say a word, but Miz Willow kept right on going.

"Every one of them families'll be farin' well now. Bryce says he reckons Logan can do the same for Daisy's lace, too. Ain't niver seen the like of what that buck's done for our holler."

Hattie got up and headed for the door. She needed to think all of this over. She mumbled a hasty good-bye to Miz Willow and waved to Daisy and Jamie, who were working in the vegetable garden. She walked as fast as she could until she came to the stream. She couldn't sit, so she paced.

He didn't abandon the holler, Hattie acknowledged ruefully. *He knew I'd be back in about a day, and Bryce was still there with Miz Willow. He knew thangs would be fine with them here. I jist felt like he'd left us behind because he wasn't home when I got back. He told me he'd had to go—that he'd done it for the holler. I didn't listen. I was too wrapped up in my own assumptions. He deserves better.*

Look at how hard he's worked to holp people around here. He's chopped enough wood to see me and Miz Willow through the winter. He went huntin' on account he knew he and Bryce et a lot of our meat. He spent time with the people of the holler and valued them for who they are and what they do, and then he took that and found a way to give them a better life. He stayed by me an' Rooster through thick and thin and showed respect to us both, even after I railed at him for his proposal.

He didn't leave us. Logan wouldn't leave me. I don't jist love him; I trust him. I had no call to say those awful things to him, and he turned the other cheek and holped me anyway. He deserves a woman who sees him for the man he is. Even though I know I was wrong, it cain never be. I still won't leave the holler, and even if he wanted to stay, I wouldn't tie him down. He should have children. We cain't ever be together, because I'm not good enough for him.

She gave herself some time to mourn her mistakes and accept that Logan would move on, then headed back to Rooster's cabin. When she got close enough to see it, she noticed Logan standing in the yard, watching her.

"Nessie's with him now. They have a few things to talk about." Logan met her halfway beneath the shade of a towering elm. "So do we."

"Yore right, Logan," Hattie looked into his intense blue eyes. "I owe you an apology. Miz Willow tole me what you done in Charleston. You tried to tell me you was lookin' after the people I care about, but I didn't listen. I misjudged you, and I'm sorry for that."

"You don't bear the blame alone, Hattie." He reached out and held her hands, sending a wave of heat through her arms. "I shouldn't have proposed until I could explain where I had been. You deserved to know everything before giving me an answer." His eyes searched hers. "Now you do. I still want you for my wife, Hattie." He raised a hand to cup her cheek. "I love you."

"I love you, too, Logan," she whispered, tears coursing down her cheeks and onto his hand. "And I know I cain trust you." She swallowed hard. "But I still cain't marry you."

"Why?" Logan demanded an answer, not budging an inch.

"I cain't go to Californy." She silently begged him to understand. "These are my people, and they need me, Logan."

"I know. Over the past months, they've become my people, too." His words sent a shiver of hope to her aching heart. "Asa, Otis, Fred, and Ted need me to follow through on the business agreements. The men of the holler came and said I'd earned a right to voice my opinion in a community vote about disassembling Rooster's still. Rooster himself cried in my arms and forsook liquor, coming back to Jesus. I can't leave them, Hattie, and I wouldn't ask you to, either."

"You mean. . ." She couldn't even voice the question.

"I want you to marry me, Hattie, and we'll stay here together." He drew her into her arms. "Say you'll love me forever."

"I cain't wed you." She pushed him away and wrapped her arms around herself to ward away the pain. "You deserve a woman who cain give you sons to carry on the Chance name. I cain't."

"Hattie." He put his arms around her once more and waited until she looked at him. "I already knew that. I want *you*. Having children isn't important to me. I have five brothers, four of whom are happily married and having babies about as fast as they can. The Chance name is well taken care of. As for me, I left Chance Ranch to find my place in the world." His arms tightened around her. "And I found it here, with you. Marry me, Hattie."

"Yes, Logan." She raised up on tiptoe to kiss him. "I love you, and I'll marry you."

"I love you, too." He smiled and spun her around. "And I've got a feeling that my adventure is just beginning."

epilogue

Dear Gideon and Miriam, Titus and Alisa, Paul and Delilah, Daniel and Lovejoy, Obie and Eunice, Hezzy and Lois, Mike and Tempy, Pollywog and Ginny Mae, and all the kids,

Sorry, but just writing all of your names took up the entire first sheet of paper, so you'll have to move on to the second one! I didn't want to leave anybody out.

Actually, we *didn't want to leave anybody out. The beautiful and all-around-wonderful Hattie Thales has agreed to marry me, Logan Chance, on the first day of fall. We know you won't make it out to the wedding, but you're in our hearts. We hope you're not mad we didn't send a telegram right away, but we figured that getting a message saying only, "Getting Hitched," would raise more questions than it was worth.*

All this means I won't be coming back to Chance Ranch. We plan to visit sometime, but Salt Lick Holler has become my home. I've found my purpose and my place here. I love you all, but I won't even pretend that I don't know you're a little relieved to hear that I'm settling down.

The truth is, you're dead wrong. Hattie's the most exciting thing that's ever happened to me, and I'll have her all to myself (except for the rest of the holler) for the rest of my life. I've become a greedy man, and I don't aim to change. Lovejoy, Hattie says to tell you that I'm the most difficult package you've ever sent, but she wouldn't have it any other way. Neither would I.

Don't worry about us. I've become a businessman of sorts between here and Charleston. Bryce will tell you all about it when he comes home—which will be late fall now instead of late summer. He's promised to stay long enough to help me build a cabin for me and Hattie.

God has been good to me, and I pray He sheds as many blessings on you. You're all in our prayers.

Love,

Logan Chance and Hattie Thales-soon-to-be-Chance

P.S. Lovejoy, your father is doing very well. He's taken down his still and come back to the Lord. He prays that you're well and asks you to write. Bryce and I decided to give him the packhorse we didn't use to replace his old mule. He and Nessie have started getting the land ready to plant corn. It's been a beautiful season for all of our lives.

A Letter To Our Readers

Dear Reader:

In order that we might better contribute to your reading enjoyment, we would appreciate your taking a few minutes to respond to the following questions. We welcome your comments and read each form and letter we receive. When completed, please return to the following:

Fiction Editor
Heartsong Presents
PO Box 719
Uhrichsville, Ohio 44683

1. Did you enjoy reading *Chance Adventure* by Kelly Eileen Hake?
   - ❑ Very much! I would like to see more books by this author!
   - ❑ Moderately. I would have enjoyed it more if

   ____

   ____

   ____

2. Are you a member of **Heartsong Presents**? ❑ Yes ❑ No
   If no, where did you purchase this book? ______________

   ____

3. How would you rate, on a scale from 1 (poor) to 5 (superior), the cover design? ______________________

4. On a scale from 1 (poor) to 10 (superior), please rate the following elements.

   ____ Heroine
   ____ Hero
   ____ Setting
   ____ Plot
   ____ Inspirational theme
   ____ Secondary characters

5. These characters were special because? ______________________

____

____

6. How has this book inspired your life? ______________________

____

____

7. What settings would you like to see covered in future **Heartsong Presents** books? ______________________

____

____

8. What are some inspirational themes you would like to see treated in future books? ______________________

____

____

9. Would you be interested in reading other **Heartsong Presents** titles? ❑ Yes ❑ No

10. Please check your age range:

❑ Under 18 ❑ 18-24
❑ 25-34 ❑ 35-45
❑ 46-55 ❑ Over 55

Name ______________________________________
Occupation ______________________________________
Address ______________________________________
City, State, Zip ______________________________________

HEARTSONG
PRESENTS

If you love Christian romance...

$10.99

You'll love Heartsong Presents' inspiring and faith-filled romances by today's very best Christian authors...DiAnn Mills, Wanda E. Brunstetter, and Yvonne Lehman, to mention a few!

When you join Heartsong Presents, you'll enjoy 4 brand-new mass market, 176-page books—two contemporary and two historical—that will build you up in your faith when you discover God's role in every relationship you read about!

Imagine...four new romances every four weeks—with men and women like you who long to meet the one God has chosen as the love of their lives...all for the low price of $10.99 postpaid.

To join, simply visit www.heartsongpresents.com or complete the coupon below and mail it to the address provided.

YES! Sign me up for Heartsong!

NEW MEMBERSHIPS WILL BE SHIPPED IMMEDIATELY!
Send no money now. We'll bill you only $10.99 postpaid with your first shipment of four books. Or for faster action, call 1-740-922-7280.

NAME ______________________________

ADDRESS ______________________________

CITY ______________ STATE _____ ZIP ______

MAIL TO: HEARTSONG PRESENTS, P.O. Box 721, Uhrichsville, Ohio 44683
or sign up at WWW.HEARTSONGPRESENTS.COM